IN THE REALM OF THE UNKNOWN

SUDHIR MENON

This book is dedicated to all those people who, in their lives, have encountered situations which have gone beyond rational and scientific explanation, to lead the concerned individuals into a sphere of total mystery , occasionally bordering on the horror side of human perception.

Contents

1

A Deadly Find

Michael Cowling was a smart, young inhabitant of one of the boroughs bordering London, called Camden. He'd been staying there ever since birth for close to thirty-five years. Unmarried, he was engaged in a printing press which his father had started over forty years ago. Now, with his dad, Peter, having called it quits on account of age and a nagging ailment, it was Michael who was holding the reins of the business and succour for the family of three. In his quiet neighbourhood, he had made a few friends over the years.

Michael's business would keep him busy for a good part of the day. There were hardly any printing presses in the vicinity of five square miles, and so business was not hard to come by. Even the ones which were five miles away were fledgling start-ups which had yet not garnered the loyal patronage that was so crucial in that kind of business. Besides, Peter had assiduously built up a huge clientele during his sunny years and so when he finally handed over the reins to Michael, the latter was vested only with the task of sustaining the success already achieved. Michael gave no cause for complaint for, with his amiable disposition and gentle manners, he had mustered a reputation of his own in the well-heeled circles of the borough.

But it was not all work and no play for Michael. He'd consolidated his good offices in the community by starting a neighbourhood block association with several like-minded individuals. They would meet up on weekends for a get-together or an outing and gradually build up their bonhomie. It was, indeed, a pleasurable place to stay and mingle.

Then, all of a sudden, the tranquility in the surrounding was shattered by a strange occurrence. James Gardiner went missing without a trace. All his folks knew was that he had gone for a walk along the by-lanes and the park, as he was wont to do, and had not returned. He was a young lad of twenty-two and well-known as a singer who had enthralled the people in the weekend get-togethers. Nobody had come forward to state that they had spotted him on the day of his disappearance. The police were informed but, in spite of applying all their investigative skills, they drew a blank, and the case was temporarily kept in abeyance as 'Unsolved'. This incident created a jolt to everyone in the otherwise serene surroundings.

Over the next couple of weeks, there were sincere efforts made by the block association members to try and console the sorrowing parents of James Gardiner who by now was near to giving up hope of ever seeing him alive again. They, nevertheless, accepted the camaraderie being exhibited in their hour of grief and gracefully thanked one and all for reaching out to them. Some, among the groups who came to meet the Gardiners, felt that probably James had fled to another part of the country where he was rumoured to have a lover of several years, the alliance with whom had not found favour with his parents. However, this matter was discussed in hush-hush tones without even a semblance of the talk reaching the ears of the grieving parents.

Another week passed by and on the approaching Tuesday, Bill Johnson, a sprightly young man of twenty-six, suddenly passed away of a massive heart attack. Now, it was the custom in the neighbourhood, that all funeral services would be conducted by the block association members; and so, in the case of Bill Johnson, too, Michael and his associates, who formed the committee managing the affairs of the association, took the lead in conducting the last rites, before the coffin was finally interred in the nearby burial ground.

At the burial, Michael noticed that most of the members had come forward to pay their last respects to the departed soul. But, in the multitude, he happened to spot an individual, a burly, though slightly elderly man, whom he had never seen before. This man was standing aloof from all the others and watching the proceedings quietly from the top of a mound. Motioning to the solitary man, Michael asked Bob Golding, one of the committee members, "Who's that, Bob?"

"Oh, that's the guy who has come to stay in house no. 21, seven houses away from yours. He's moved in a month ago, after the Sinclairs left for Australia," replied Bob nonchalantly. "I don't know his name though and have never met him personally."

"I see," said Michael, mentally making a note to meet the man after the funeral ceremony was over.

The burial having taken place, the crowd began to disperse. Michael looked around for the elderly man, but he was nowhere to be seen. Maybe, he had left before the ceremony got over, but Michael didn't give the matter another thought.

Life returned to normal over the next couple of weeks and then, five days later, another calamity struck the neighbourhood. This time, it was Charlie Watson who had gone missing. Charlie was a college-going lad of twenty years and a face known for his docile temperament. He had left home in the evening to buy groceries in one of the supermarkets and was expected to return before dusk. However, even with dusk having passed and darkness having descended, there was no sign of Charlie. His parents made frantic calls to the residences of all his known friends but he had not gone to visit any of them. The supermarket from where he had done his purchases, reported that he had left around six in the evening. So, where did he go? This was the question in everyone's minds and soon the matter reached the ears of Michael.

There was an impromptu meeting of the committee members where there was a consensus that the latest disappearance was not a coincidence and that something was seriously amiss in the neighbourhood. The committee nominated Michael and two others to conduct their own probe into the mystery and come up with their findings in a couple of weeks.

Meanwhile, the police came and did their investigation but, like in the earlier case, there was no progress and they kept the matter in cold storage till some clue emerged which could throw light into the entire episode.

The next day, Michael decided to take a walk alongside the row of houses abutting his bungalow. It was a sunny day and the heaps of dead leaves all around, signified the advent of spring. The chirping of birds and the scampering of an occasional squirrel caught the fancy of Michael, as he trudged along on the paved sidewalk. He reached house no. 21 and saw the elderly man pottering around his garden with his lawnmower. He caught the man's gaze and waved out to him, but the latter looked away and did not reciprocate. In fact, he did not look again in his direction. 'That's strange' thought Michael, as he continued walking further. On his way back, he went to meet the families of house nos. 20 & 22 and in the deliberations that he had, he was given to understand that the elderly man was not social and had not interacted with them in any way. In fact, neither did they know his name nor whether he had any other folks in his house. Michael found all this feedback to be intriguing but he let it pass for the moment and returned to his house, in time for a brunch before he left for his press.

On the way, Michael was constantly seized with what he had heard about the elderly man from his immediate neighbours, as well as his own experience of the man. 'Why would he behave in the manner that he did? After all, the neighbourhood was a close-knit community with all its inhabitants ever willing to help each other,' thought Michael, as he entered his work-place and took stock of the progress on the orders for the day.

The weekend was coming and Michael decided he'd break the ice with the elderly man by inviting him for the get-together. So, on Friday morning itself, Michael made his way to the metal gate which secured the property around house no. 21. He rang the bell mounted on a pillar outside, and in response the automated gate opened inwards to let him in. There didn't seem to be any semblance of life around, nor any sounds from within the house. Michael walked up the small driveway and climbed the three steps in front of the main door. Before he could ring the doorbell, the door opened and remained a little ajar. "Come on in," said a voice from within.

Michael gently pushed the door so that he could enter and took a step inside. There was no one in the hall but, from an adjacent room, a voice said, "Please be seated. Will be with you in a minute." Michael sat down on a chair placed in the corner and looked round the hall. There wasn't much furniture but the windows had heavy drapes that was probably meant to shut off sunlight completely. There was an odd smell that hit his nostrils but he couldn't fathom from where it came. Some strange-looking masks were perched at irregular intervals on the walls from where these frowned or grimaced violently at the 'guests' who would be seated below. Michael began to feel a tad uncomfortable. Such 'hospitality' was definitely not envisaged and he waited with bated breath to meet the elderly man whose voice it was that he had heard thus far.

Soon, the burly elderly man came from an adjacent room at one end. Michael stood up and extended his hand which was accepted with full gusto. Michael winced with pain as his hand was clasped with a grip that could probably have bent a piece of metal, he thought. The man gave an awkward grin seeing the effect of the handshake on Michael's face. "Birkman is my name. Sam Birkman. So, what brings you here?" enquired the man, as Michael glanced at his palm to check for any possible damage that might have occurred in the show of introduction.

"My name's Michael Cowling. I'm the president of the neighbourhood block association. The association hosts weekend get-togethers and outings and it's a great opportunity to meet up and share all the latest news and views. In this regard, I've come to invite you for the get-together to be held on Sunday at 6.00 p.m. sharp."

"That's very kind of you. I would have loved to attend but have another engagement already lined up. Hopefully, another time."

"But you could send your family, I suppose."

"I stay here alone," said the man, looking at Michael straight in the eye.

"Oh, I see. Then I'll take leave of you and hope to catch up with you some other time."

"That'll be fine. But pray, please be seated for a while. I've made some cheesecake which I would like you to savour."

"Probably, some other time. I must go now."

"But I insist, you must partake of the dessert," countered the man with steely decisiveness.

"Well, if you insist, I shall." So, Michael sat down again, as Sam Birkman made a quick retreat, presumably to the kitchen.

Now, one could say it was fate or pure luck that came Michael's way, that he happened to sight a mirror kept on a mantelpiece. Michael looked at the mirror and saw a certain reflection in it. It was the door of an adjoining room which was ajar and through it he could see, though not clearly, that something was kept on a table. He tiptoed towards the room and looked in. What beheld him almost knocked him out of his senses. There, on the floor of the room were two long deep freezers about 7 feet by 4 feet. Next to these, on two tables were laid out the bodies of James Gardiner and Charlie Watson! A quick glance of the two bodies showed that barring the heads, all other parts were thoroughly mutilated and even the entrails had been pulled out. A bloodstained large hacksaw and a kitchen knife lay nearby which bore testimony to the horrendous crime.

"So, you've seen it, have you?" bellowed Sam Birkman, somewhere from behind, as Michael moved aside at this sudden outburst. He could not have been an instant too soon, for just as he had moved away, Sam brought down a heavy club to smash Michael's head. He missed his target, lost balance and fell flat on the floor, with the club flying off his hand and falling where Michael now stood. Michael instinctively picked it up and landed a massive blow on Sam's left knee such that the burly man was squirming with excruciating pain. The latter hurled some invectives at Michael who beat a hasty retreat and with one quick jerk of the handle of the main door, he opened it and ran out, followed by Sam. Michael's athletic body and fitness regimen came in handy, for he scaled Sam's gate in a jiffy and was on his way home, before Sam could anywhere come close to getting hold of him.

Once inside, Michael, still panting from the trauma of the ghastly episode, immediately called the cops and narrated the entire story. The cops were quick on their heels but Sam had bolted in the meantime. There was a thickly wooded forest which housed a high-walled tiger reserve about five miles away and it was believed that Sam must have headed in that direction to ward off imminent capture. The police were hot on his trail and had sealed off all escape routes. They reached the forest in good time and checked with the reserve wardens whether anyone had climbed the wall and jumped in. There had been no such intrusion according to a quick verification that was conducted.

On the third day after this episode, Sam's bloated body was found floating in a canal nearby, and was washed ashore. The people of the neighbourhood heaved a sigh of relief. After a brief spell, when the grieving was over, the inhabitants were at least convinced that there was a closure of the two missing persons cases and in due course, life, once again, returned to normal. But the memory of the

demon and cannibal that was Sam Birkman, continued to haunt the tranquil neighbourhood for a long time to come.
THE END

2

A Traumatic Encounter

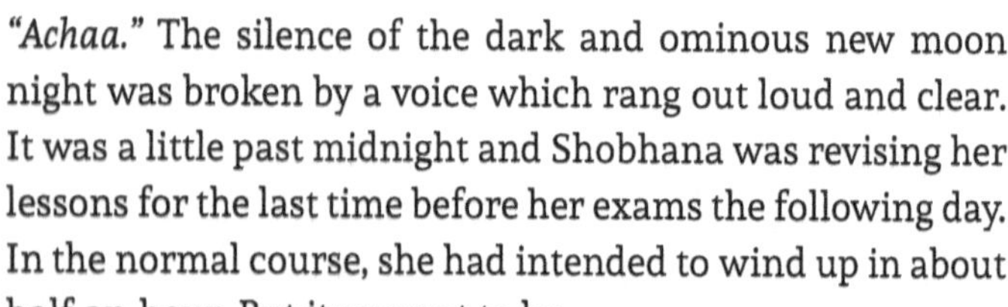

"*Achaa.*" The silence of the dark and ominous new moon night was broken by a voice which rang out loud and clear. It was a little past midnight and Shobhana was revising her lessons for the last time before her exams the following day. In the normal course, she had intended to wind up in about half-an-hour. But it was not to be.

In the large household, consisting of her parents, siblings, uncles and aunts, it was, indeed, past bedtime. But the shrillness of the scream shattered even the boundaries of a relatively loud bark of a dog.

Govindan Nair was quick on his toes. The voice was unmistakably that of his daughter. The scream was fraught with some perceived danger, as he surmised, while he picked up the large torchlight and a lantern. In the several decades gone by, electrification in remote rural villages in Kerala was yet to take place. As was his custom, a baton dangled from his hip and he decided to arm himself additionally with a sword.

"Where are you going?" queried Thangamma, in a crisp tone. Her sound sleep had been disturbed by the movements of her husband, searching for whatever he wanted to carry with him.

"Didn't you hear the cry of our daughter?"

"No, I didn't."

"Her scream seemed to have come from the hall in the basement," continued Govindan. In a jiffy, he was out of his bedroom and running towards the stairs leading to the basement. He was joined by his brother, Peetambharan, who had also heard Shobhana's scream. The two men made their way down the winding stairway, with Govindan holding the lantern before him.

His daughter's scream seemed to resonate in his ears as Govindan and his brother reached the landing at the bottom. The door to the hall was open. It was dark inside. Govindan gave his brother the lantern while he shone the torch around the vast hall. In the centre was a large rectangular table with several chairs on either side. This place was used by the family as a dining hall as well as to entertain guests. At one end of the table, a chair seemed to have been moved backwards in a diagonal manner, indicating that someone who had been probably seated there, had tried to leave in a hurry. Govindan flashed his torch in the area around the chair and lo and behold, the body of his daughter lay spreadeagled on the wooden flooring.

"There she is," exclaimed Govindan, as he quickly moved towards her. Peetambharan followed him and held the lantern as he knelt down to pick up his daughter. Govindan felt she was running a high temperature, as her body was very warm. She was obviously unconscious, as she did not respond to her name being called.

With a quick jerk, Govindan lifted thirteen-year-old Shobhana and proceeded to move towards the doorway and up the stairs, Peetambharan in tow.

By now, other members of the household had woken up, with the word having been passed around that something was amiss with Shobhana. Some were in the drawing room while others loitered in the corridor. Suddenly, there was silence amongst them as they perceived Govindan coming up the stairs with Shobhana.

"What's the matter with her," wailed Thangamma, as he ran towards her husband.

"Nothing much, I hope. She's running a temperature. Seems, something must have upset her as there are indications that she tried to leave the hall in a hurry. She's lost consciousness, so we won't know until she regains it. Now, we need to immediately get her medical attention."

"Maybe, she's just fainted. Let me see if I can revive her by sprinkling some water on her face." Saying this, Thangamma ran to the kitchen to get a tumbler of water. She sprinkled it liberally over her daughter's face and sure enough, in a moment, her daughter made some movement and gradually opened her eyes.

There was a loud cheer and clapping from the assemblage as they craned their necks to look at the little girl. "Give her some breathing space. She needs it now," said Govindan, as he moved his hand to signal for some space in the area where the girl lay. "What happened, my dear? Why did you scream?" asked Govindan, softly to his daughter.

His daughter, in response, mumbled something and then burst into sobs, uncontrollably. Govindan lifted her and placed her head on his shoulder. "Don't worry, my dear, whatever it was that made you scream, we'll get it sorted out." Then, motioning to Peetambharan, he asked, "Could you join me on my way to meet Dr. Sahadevan?"

"For sure, goes without saying," replied Peetambharan almost immediately.

"Fine then, we'll set forth at once," Govindan was emphatic.

As the two men and the girl set out in the dark, the householders trained their eyes to observe their silhouettes until they disappeared around a bend leading to the main road. Dr. Sahadevan's residence was nearby and he was always accessible to the villagers at any time of day and night when he was not at his clinic, a couple of Km away.

"Sorry that we are disturbing you at this unearthly hour, doctor, but my daughter had lost consciousness and is also having a high temperature. Could you please attend to her?" entreated Govindan, as the doctor himself opened the door of his modest bungalow.

"Sure. Bring her in."

Once inside, the doctor asked Govindan, "What happened?"

"I really don't know, doctor," said Govindan apologetically and then proceeded to narrate everything from the time he had heard his daughter scream.

The doctor heard him soberly and was pensive as he put on his stethoscope and took the girl's blood pressure and felt her pulse. He then took her temperature and patted the girl on her cheek. Then taking Govindan by the hand towards a corner of the room, he stated, "Your daughter has apparently gone through some trauma because of fright."

"Fright, doctor?" Govindan was wide-eyed.

"Yes. There was something which had caused her to be frightened and hence the fainting and high temperature. But, not to worry. I'll give her some tablets and a tonic and hopefully she'll be okay in a couple of days. However, she should take complete rest for a week. But you need to ensure that she must not be left alone even for a second till she recovers fully. Is that understood?"

"Yes, doctor," said Govindan, feeling reassured that nothing drastically was wrong. Then reaching for his shirt pocket, he searched for twenty-five rupees to be given to the doctor as his fees, when the latter held his hand and restrained him from doing so.

"That's okay. You can pay me some other time. For the moment, we need to nurse your child back to health. She must not attend any exam till she is perfectly fine." Govindan nodded in confirmation.

"Thank you, doctor, for your timely help. Good night." The two men and the child then took leave of Dr. Sahadevan.

On the way home, Dr. Sahadevan's diagnosis of his daughter's condition caused him to reflect on one particular word – fright. 'What possibly could have caused his daughter to be afraid'? he wondered.

Back home, the householders were waiting patiently for all news. They were relieved when they saw the small party trooping in.

"Tell me, what did the doctor say?" queried Thangamma.

Govindan revealed what the doctor had stated and then there was a hushed silence all around. Trauma on account of fright – what in blazes did that mean. The householders seemed perplexed. As an instant remedy, they unanimously suggested that the basement be locked immediately, till there was clarity in the matter. Govindan and Thangamma nodded in agreement.

Now, Govindan Nair had bought the spacious bungalow about six months ago from the earlier owner, Narayan Kartha for a relatively low price. There were other properties available in the vicinity, but for some reason best known to Govindan Nair, he preferred to buy the house where he was currently staying. Several of his friends and potential neighbours, when made aware of his intention to buy the property, cautioned him from doing so, stating that the place was haunted, but Govindan Nair was resolute in his decision. An avowed iconoclast, he likewise did not give any credence to supernatural occurrences.

According to people in the know, the story about the place was that in a century gone by, an *adivasi* girl was abducted and molested on a new moon night by some influential upper caste men who owned the property in question. She was left in an unconscious state behind some shrubs in a wooded area close to the property. On regaining consciousness, she walked to the nearest railway track and jumped in front of a speeding train but not before she had cursed her assailants and all those who occupied the property. While the men went scot-free, the curse of the dead woman prevailed in the vicinity where the hideous crime was committed. Time and again, thereafter, when several families came to stay in the property, they experienced unearthly events which was beyond any rational explanation. One by one, over the years, families quit the place after which the house lay vacant for a long time before it was purchased by Narayan Kartha. The latter and his family, also, had an extremely horrific stay in the house, although they preferred not to talk much about it to people.

Meanwhile, Shobhana was well on the path to recovery. Thangamma, Karthiyani, Indira and Sulochana took turns in ensuring that she was never left alone. They attended to all her needs and made the girl gradually return to normalcy. Everyone in the house was relieved at the progress of the child and thanked the Almighty for fructifying their prayers. Many in the household, curious to know what had transpired with Shobhana, asked her in the coming weeks, what was it that had frightened her on that fateful night, but the child seemed resolute as ever, not to divulge what she had kept privy to herself.

It was about a month, thereafter, on a wintry evening that Govindan made his daughter sit beside him to ask her thus, "Tell me my dear, do you remember what is it that troubled you in the basement on that fateful night?"

Shobhana's face was a picture of fright. She held her father's hand in her clasp and tried to utter something but words did not emanate from her quivering lips.

"Take it easy, my dear. There's nothing to worry. I am always there to help you. You can tell me with confidence. I will find a solution to the problem."

For some time, the girl looked blankly at the space before her till she gained strength to face her father and tell her story. And, this was what she had to tell.

"*Achaa*, as you were aware, I had gone down to the basement to revise the lessons for my exam the next day. Since it was a relatively quiet part of the house, I felt I would not be disturbed. I had taken a couple of lit candles to facilitate my reading and then had settled down to read my lessons. It was, indeed, very quiet all around, except for the sound of crickets. I must have spent about half-an-hour reading when all of a sudden, the candle lights began to flicker violently. I passed my palm around the flame to steady it, although there was no breeze blowing and that was the time that my eyes rested on a form at the other end of the table." Shobhana began to shake with fear but her father comforted her with soothing words. Nevertheless, she stared ahead of her as if looking at someone or something. Her father looked in the direction she was looking but saw only a wall. Suddenly, Shobhana began to sob uncontrollably and covered her face on her father's lap, all the while clasping his hand tightly. Govindan stroked her hair and tried to reassure her that everything would be fine. Her father's support helped Shobhana to dispel her fears, as she continued, "The form was that of a woman. She was black in colour, stark naked from the waist upwards and had large blood-shot eyes. Her tongue was thrust out, as if baying for blood. Her hair was long and fell over her shoulders and her hands were resting on the table. Her gaze was fixed on me. A slow moan seemed to emanate from the woman which was not only horrifying to say the least but also accentuated the entire ominous scenario that was created. My whole body was shivering with fright and I could not utter a word. A strange feeling rose along my spine and the hair on my arms were standing on end. The next moment, however, I screamed, hoping that you would be able to come for help and as I pushed my chair backwards and decided to run, I tripped and fell. I do not know what transpired thereafter." Shobhana stopped in her monologue and looked at her father who had been listening attentively. His face was grave and he did not say a word. "Who do you think must have been that woman, *achaa*, and where did she come from and go thereafter?" Shobhana was curious to know.

"I do not know, my dear," replied her father, pensively. Then, rising from his chair, he said, "Let's go inside. Probably, dinner is getting ready."

Govindan was not one to be taken in by such occurrences had it happened to him. However, since it was involving his daughter, for whom it seemed that the incident had left an indelible mark in her memory, he decided to take remedial action to avoid a repetition of the same.

Later, that night, Govindan apprised his wife of what his daughter had told him.

"For sure, it must have been the ghost of the *adivasi* woman who had been violated in a century gone by," opined Thangamma.

"It's quite possible," responded Govindan, without a second thought. Between them, they decided that the hunt for a new house would begin the following day. They agreed to keep the story under wraps and also to conduct some *puja* to ward off evil spirits.

And so, the curtain once more seemed to have fallen on the queer happenings at the spacious bungalow, at least for some time to come, till probably some other bold individual came by to make the place his residence.

THE END

<u>GLOSSARY</u>
1)*Achaa* : father
2)*Adivasi* : a lower caste tribal

3

A Trip Goes Awry

It was the advent of spring. Gagan and family lived in a hilly tract in Uttarakand, a northern state in India. Their modest home commanded a beautiful view of the landscape with its lush green slopes, abundant trees with bright green leaves, a vast expanse of bushes and shrubs, a rivulet wending its way through the gorges and fresh saplings and plants that were beginning to spring up everywhere with many of these already showing signs of flowering. Certain other plants which had already been growing through winter now shone in full bloom, gently swaying in the cool mountain breeze. Flowers of all hues lined the wayside and the burgeoning growth of flora all around gave out an odour of fresh vegetation. Patches of white clouds resembling small tufts of cotton wafted in the breeze as these kissed the topmost branches and foliage of some trees that dotted the mountainside. The early morning mist settled down as dewdrops on the leaves like so many clear beads which later on, as the sun rose in the sky, coalesced and dripped onto the shrubs below. The early morning birds chirped loudly in unison exuding a wanton display of total abandon. Occasionally, one of the finer coloured birds would hop from one branch onto another, as the feathered flock played their little games which were always a treat to watch.

Gagan was an early riser. After getting into slacks and walking shoes, he set out for his regular morning walk which would take him round the bend and down a black-topped road which sloped marginally till it plateaued out at the junction where a post office was situated. Thereafter, the road would take him to the bus station and the police *chowky* or kiosk,and further on to a restaurant and a grocery store. From there he would retrace his steps and reach in good time to savour the piping hot breakfast churned out by his wife, Urmila, even while the kids were still contemplating in bed whether it was time for them to wake up.

But that day was different. It was a Sunday but even so he made his son and daughter wake up and asked them to get ready soon for the day ahead, which would take them all on a hike after walking across a bridge about five km away. The children did as per their father's instructions because they were excited to go on the hike which involved crossing a bridge. They had undergone many hikes before but this was the first time that a bridge was in the picture. Very soon Urmila packed all the backpacks with the requisite amount of food and then Gagan got his personal bag of implements and instruments ready. After the children had a quick breakfast, they were all set to go in their car which would take them to one end of the bridge.

It was still quite chilly at 8.00 a.m. when they hit the road. The kids, Pawan and Ambika were chattering with excitement as the sheer thought of crossing a fairly long bridge with a deep gorge below between two hills evoked mixed feelings of ecstasy and trepidation in their young minds. The road towards the bridge involved driving up an incline with a few hair-pin bends. Gagan negotiated the narrow road with the mastery of an experienced driver for, over the years, he had taken to driving as a fish takes to water. The family finally reached an open area where a space was allotted for parking cars. His was the third car in the parking area, which meant there were already two groups or families who had crossed the bridge and were on the opposite hill.

The family alighted and slung their back packs as they surveyed the bridge and the hill beyond. In winter, the hill would have been snow-capped but now with spring having set in, the hillside bore a green hue from the myriads of trees and vegetation and even from the hill across, it presented a spectacle of being fairly thickly wooded. But Gagan was not worried about the relatively foreboding nature of the hill and he knew that should any wild animal attack them on their way, he had a licenced and loaded revolver to take care of all such eventualities. The family made their way towards the bridge which was not exactly a steel structure but made of coir and some strong fibre which could resist the weight of at least twenty people crossing over at a time. Having now reached it, Gagan took the lead with the children behind him and his wife making up the rear. Gagan advised his family to break step as they crossed the bridge and not to look below lest they should feel giddy. The others obliged and after a suspenseful ten minutes or so, the family had crossed over to the other side.

Everyone heaved a sigh of relief and then Gagan with a wave of his hand, signalled to the others to follow him. There were very clear pathways made out to facilitate hikers and Gagan took one of them. As he proceeded, he felt the gradient gradually increasing till after a climb of about thirty minutes, the party sat down at a clearing to take a breather. Besides Gagan, who had been an athletic champion in his school and college days, Urmila, too, had taken well to athletics in her younger days. The children were also adept at games and sports and so the family was able to take the rigours of a hiking expedition with a fair deal of confidence and enthusiasm. After a gap of ten minutes, they again trudged up the incline, till after a good forty-five minutes or so they had reached the top of the hill, where they saw the other hikers who had preceded them, relaxing and playing some games. Some were engaged in a photography session as the panoramic view presented an ideal setting for a group photograph.

Gagan smiled at a gentleman who waved out to him and soon he had introduced himself and his family members to all the people around, who invited them to partake of the aromatic food that was generously displayed on a foldable table. All in all, they were fourteen in number and so in this small band of people, the bonhomie quickly built up through the food and games and, of course, the exchange of news and views. Apart from the family, the others were not locals and had come from Chattisgarh on a vacation. They had a tight schedule and were set to depart from the location immediately after an early lunch, which was about an hour away. Gagan and family enjoyed the company of the visitors and joined them in partaking of the lunch which included the food that Urmila had packed. During the conversation that ensued, they came to know that their mobiles would not work in the location as there was a serious network problem. Gagan did not envisage an issue to crop up on account of this as his home was anyway, only 5 km away from the location.

After lunch, the other group bade farewell to the family after exchanging contact numbers, with a promise to meet again should there be an occasion for the family to go anytime to Chattisgarh. Gagan said he and his family would stay on till about 5.00 p.m., as they had planned to spend the day there.

It was a bit quiet after the group had left but the family spent their time scouting around the peak of the hill which by all accounts was quite a large area. They took photographs, played some board games and then took a short nap, before deciding to return home.

So at around 4.30 p.m., the family packed up and then began the descent along the same path they had come. This was obviously much easier and less strenuous than the uphill trek and so they were almost at the foothill within thirty-five minutes. The bridge could be seen in the distance and they made their way rapidly towards it. And then before their very eyes, a huge tree seemed to block their vision. Before they knew it, they heard a deafening sound that reverberated through the gorge before them and then there was an eerie silence. Gagan took stock of the situation and realized that a tree at the foothill overlooking the gorge had been uprooted and had fallen over the bridge which, as a consequence, did not exist anymore!

It took some time for the stark truth to sink into the minds of the family: they were cut-off from proceeding any further and any hopes of reaching their car died even before they were kindled. They reached the foothill and surveyed the devastation before them. One end of the bridge had totally disappeared and the other on the opposite side was resting against some rocks about fifteen metres into the gorge.

The children looked at Urmila who in turn gazed dazedly at Gagan. Nobody spoke. It was as if everyone had lost their power of speech and the saliva had dried in all their mouths. Then after a few seconds, Gagan said, "I think we're staying put. There is no other way to reach our car. We will have to spend at least the night here before we can hope for some help tomorrow."

Ambika, who was only ten years old, broke into tears and started crying inconsolably. Urmila went to her side and tried to comfort her. Gagan stood stoically beside his family, his eyes trained towards the sky. He had sometimes seen a helicopter flying near his home and banked upon such a chance occurrence to lift them out of the morass. But look as he might, there was not a sound which pierced the silence of the hill.

The sun had now begun to sink lower in the western horizon as its lengthy rays bathed the slopes of the foothill. In another twenty minutes or so, it would become dark and then the family would be at the mercy of the unknown. They had not explored the entire hill to assess whether any wild life existed nor were they confident that the foothill was indeed the safest place on the hill to spend the night.

Gagan took out his binoculars from his bag of implements and accessories and scanned the opposite side from where they had come to see if there was any semblance of any movement but there was none. Nobody in their right senses would have come to the hill late in the evening and, once again, Gagan told himself that he and his family were temporarily cut off. The next day being a Monday and a working day, no locals would come for a trek and he could only hope for some help from vacationers who might decide to come to the hill. If only the mobile network issue could get resolved, he thought.

The hillside blocked the last rays of the sun and darkness finally descended over the area. Gagan took out the torch from his bag and shone it around them. He identified a clearing on the right side and he directed the rest to follow him. They spread the mats which they had brought with them and used their knapsacks as their pillows. Since there was nothing else to do they lay down and as they gazed above, the stars sparkled in their heavenly abode. Nobody was feeling sleepy for the sudden change of fortunes and the prospect of having to spend the night on the hill kept their minds alert. Nobody was feeling hungry either because their predicament had driven out the pangs of hunger from their bellies. Besides, there was nothing left of the food in the knapsacks, as everything had been consumed while they were atop the hill. It was indeed a most unenviable situation.

As the night wore on, slumber gradually overtook the family as they curled up on the mats, sans any blankets to protect them from the cold or any sort of tent or closed enclosure to ward off the insects and other creatures. It was very peaceful and quiet on the terrain with a pristine breeze blowing over their faces.

Aoowooooooh! What was that? Gagan got up with a start as did the others. The sound was loud and clear and pierced the silence that had nestled all around. Gagan looked at his watch. It was 2.35 a.m. Some animal on the prowl, perhaps, thought Gagan but there was no way of knowing. A bird flapped its wings and flew off from a tree in front of them to another perch. An owl flew swiftly and low over their heads. Ambika ran towards Urmila and held her tight to quell her fright. Gagan moved towards some dry leaves which were lying at the foot of a tree and brought a cluster enclosed by his arms. He laid it down a few feet away from the others and then with a lighter from his bag, Gagan lit the pile of leaves. The dried leaves crackled as the fire spread through the heap and Gagan and Pawan collected another heap of leaves and twigs to keep it burning. The fire provided warmth to the family but more importantly, it was designed to ward off any animal that could be in the vicinity. As his wife and children strained their eyes into the darkness of the wooded area all around to locate any possible movement, Gagan nervously toyed with the revolver, should it come in handy.

It was a tiresome and needless wait for something to happen. None of them wanted to take any chances as the darkness through which even the light from the heavenly bodies did not seem to permeate did not provide any answers to their fear of the unknown. Urmila opened a flask and poured out the remnants of coffee to the children, who washed it down in a jiffy. Anything was welcome at this juncture to dissuade the senses from being wary of the source of the sound. Gagan suggested that the others get some sleep while he stood guard. There was no point for all of them to be awake all together; but sleep was the last thing on the minds of Urmila and the kids. "If you remain awake, we will all join you," said Urmila resolutely. Any amount of cajoling by Gagan did not cause her to change her decision, as she remarked, "We're all in it together, so let's all face the danger, whatever it is, together."

Gagan did not argue. He knew his wife better than anyone else. A massive flapping of wings by another bird startled the small group as they sat together in a huddle waiting for the morn to break. *Aoowooooooh!* There it was again, loud and clear. Urmila and the kids froze with fright as this time Gagan was able to surmise that the sound seemed to come from the area before them, for loud though it was, it had an echo which reverberated through the woods and seemed to percolate all the way with a sinister urgency. Gagan pacified his family to stay calm and reassured them that no danger would come to them. He looked long and hard at the darkness in front of him but there was no sign to indicate even the slightest of movement. Should he fire in the air to frighten away whatever animal was causing the sound? He decided that would not help, for it might only draw the creature closer to them. A vigil was the best thing in the circumstances and that is what he intended to do.

A rustle among the shrubs once again put the family on full watch but they felt relieved when they saw a mongoose scurrying away with a snake in its mouth. With not having had any dinner and practically no sleep, the weariness was taking its toll on the children, as they dug their heads in Urmila's lap, who, incidentally, was keeping a vigil along with her husband. What ill omen had brought them to this fate, she thought as she rubbed her eyes with her palms to refrain from dozing off.

The sky was beginning to change its hue as the first rays of light shot through the darkness. Very soon, the sun would creep up from behind the hill and bring with it new hope for the stranded hikers. Hopefully, there would be someone who would come to trek up the hill and then they would be able to spot them from across the gorge. Such were the thoughts that traversed the optimistic minds of the adults as they patiently waited for the break of dawn. Gagan, once again, looked at his mobile and never felt so helpless in his life.

Dawn broke over the hills within the next thirty minutes and the scene around them changed drastically. What felt to be ominous and foreboding throughout the night, now looked fresh and inviting to be explored. Gagan was deep in thought. He needed to get his family out of this quagmire as soon as possible, but how was he to go about it without a mobile phone to assist him, he wondered. He began to scout around to see if there was anything of help that would be lying there. He found a plastic tumbler and he picked it up. He shouted 'hello' into it and the echo of his voice reverberated through the gorge. This will do, he thought, to attract the attention of anyone across the gorge. He could see his car as he had parked it the day before. If only there was some way to reach it.

The children woke up from their slumber and quickly adjusted to the new environs. They were hungry and tired but did not reveal their plight to their parents. Gagan continued to walk around to see if he could spot some fruit trees but there was no luck waiting for him. He came back to the clearing and decided to wait. The early morning birds created a burst of chirrups and screeches that often reached a crescendo, even though it was a welcome sound to hear. Gagan decided to gather another big pile of dry leaves and twigs to attract attention, should they see any sign of life or movement in the coming hours.

It was now 8.00 a.m. As he had thought earlier, it being a working day, the likelihood of any locals coming to the hill was very slim so he crossed his fingers hoping that some vacationers would show up. And then an idea struck him. Why not maintain a steady fire burning throughout the time they were there? It would attract the attention of any helicopter that may happen to be passing by or scouring the area. It was a possibility but not an eventuality. He needed to explore all options and this indeed was one of them. So he instructed Pawan to follow him such that neither was out of earshot of Urmila and Ambika; and the duo collected enough grass, leaves and timber within the ensuing hour that would keep a fire burning for at least five hours. And this time they were in luck, for Pawan spotted a guava hanging from a tree. He shouted out to his father and then Gagan saw a number of guavas hanging low from the tree, ready to be plucked. The father son collected quite a few guavas and returned to hand them over to Urmila and Ambika. With at least their hunger pangs being attended to for the time being, Gagan concentrated on the task at hand, viz. sending smoke signals in the hope that it would be noticed. He lit the fire and a steady pall of smoke rose above the tree-tops and beyond. It was a bright and sunny day and, against the blue sky, the smoke was sure to be seen. Gagan sat back and decided to take some rest, while Urmila and the kids kept vigil. After a power nap of thirty minutes, Gagan surveyed the area opposite the gorge through his binoculars. There was still no sign of life and no way to communicate to the world across. He was beginning to despair but he held his composure because, should he have wilted, he would have broken the morale of his family.

Gagan went to the edge of the gorge and looked down. The gorge was steep and deep and there was no chance for anyone, be it even an experienced mountaineer, to descend and then climb up from the other side. He, therefore, set aside even the notion of trying to get help by that method.

The day wore on and still there was no sign of any hikers. Urmila and the children were beginning to show signs of despair but Gagan held his cool. Just as he was about to resign to the possibility of having to spend one more night on the hill, he heard the whirr of a helicopter and immediately looked skywards. A helicopter was approaching them as it must have seen the smoke rising above the hill. Gagan took out his shirt and started waving frantically to the crew of the helicopter. Apparently, they saw him and the helicopter descended to the level of the foothill but was stationary above the gorge. In the ensuing cacophony of the sounds of the helicopter, Gagan explained the situation and showed them the clearing in the woods where they could descend. The crew signalled thumbs up to them and before long they had landed in the clearing. Gagan and family squeezed into the helicopter and were soon airborne. The helicopter landed near the car park and then, after thanking the crew profusely, Gagan and family were homeward bound in their car.

Totally relieved on having ended their ordeal, the family, nevertheless, learnt a couple of lessons. They would never again venture into a place where there was no mobile network coverage and never have to cross a bridge to reach their destination.

But the mysterious sound in the night which had instilled fear in them was enough reason to cause them to shudder for many more nights to come.

THE END

4

A Tryst With The Dead

Sara's fleeting eyes picked up the multitude of people in the sprawling metro station. There were college-going kids, working women, men in overpowering numbers and, of course, a sprinkling of tourists. Nobody particularly whom she knew or had seen before seemed to be present on the platform with whom she could have spent time during her relatively long journey to the terminus. As she trained her vision to check for the oncoming train, her eyes fell on an old lady dressed in a long frock, all wrinkled with age and steadying her gait with a walking stick which had a flat base. At the very instant that Sara saw her, the lady, too, lifted her gaze and spied her. She smiled involuntarily and looked friendly, but she had steely eyes with a piercing look that made Sara shudder momentarily. 'Must be a strict disciplinarian', thought Sara, as she got ready to board the train, which had just then pulled into the station. Clusters of humans fell out of the train as, simultaneously, people pushed gently in a bid to board before the whistle went off for the doors to close.

The train moved out of the station and Sara got a place to stand in between the two rows of seats on either side of her. 'Quite crowded', she thought for a weekday, as a college student in front of her made a random movement over ninety degrees. His backpack, almost covering his entire back and bulging with a plethora of articles, hit her across the face and sent her momentarily of balance. "I'm terribly sorry," he said, as Sara gathered herself, mildly nursing her face in the region where the offending bag had struck her.

"That's okay," she replied, trying to play down the incident. "It's at least redeeming to know that you are aware of the consequence of your action, inadvertent though it may be, because the movements of a backpack do not generally relay the effects it has on humans, other than the one carrying it," continued Sara with a smile. The college student gave her a sheepish look, one that told her that the boy was genuinely sorry.

The train bolted down the track and then made a mild turn towards the right, which sent most of the standees in the compartment leaning over towards the left. Sara, too, was one of them. 'Newton's Third Law in action' she told herself, as the train reached the next station. A number of people tumbled out and almost an equal number or more entered the compartment. In the process, some seats which had fallen vacant were quickly filled up. Sara made an attempt to reach a seat about five feet away from her, but a portly lady who had boarded just then, made an aggressive bid and cornered the seat for herself. 'Too bad', thought Sara. 'Guess I'm destined to stand throughout my journey', she told herself. Now, in her rush for the seat, she had moved about five paces ahead and she now had a strange feeling that she was being observed. Guardedly, she made furtive glances around her and then her eyes met those of the old lady she had seen at the time of boarding. The lady, once again, smiled at her and this time she smiled back. 'Did she know her? Had she seen her before?' Sara's thoughts tended to be disoriented as she moved a little towards the front in order to take cover behind a burly man. She, somehow, felt uncomfortable looking at those eyes of the old lady.

Seven more stations went by and Sara was still standing. A toddler was asleep on her mother's lap and for some time, Sara fixed her gaze on the innocence of that face. "Would you like to sit, my dear? You've been standing for quite some time now." The voice seemed to come from a few feet away, but it was soft and clear. Sara looked in the direction of the voice and saw the old lady beckoning her.

"Oh, thank you, but I don't mind standing," replied Sara, rather nervously.

"You cannot be standing the whole length of your journey, child. I insist you take my seat, even if it is for a few minutes. It would rest those tired legs of yours," countered the old lady, with a rather determined look.

Sara felt embarrassed that she had to unseat the old lady. But the insistence of the lady was more overpowering than the embarrassment that she felt and she quickly settled down in the old lady's seat. 'That's a good girl," exclaimed the lady with a twinkle in her eyes which gave Sara some respite from her gaze.

The train rolled into the next station and as luck would have it for the old lady, the person sitting next to Sara alighted, and then the seat was occupied by the senior citizen. "So, where are you off to?" she asked Sara.

"Till the terminus," replied Sara.

"Oh, but that's where I'm also headed," stated the old lady, who introduced herself as Natalie.

"I'm Sara."

"That's a nice name. I had a distant relative by the same name. So, what do you do?"

"I'm a primary school teacher," replied Sara.

"Do you have any of your folks staying at the terminus?"

"Yes, indeed. My aunt has been staying there for the past ten years and I'm going now to visit her."

"Oh, I see."

Sara was cautious not to ask the old lady any questions that might infuriate her, so she kept a studied silence.

"Do you like some gummy bears?" asked Natalie.

"No, thank you, but I'm not a person who likes sweets."

Natalie shrugged her shoulders and popped in a couple of the chewies into her mouth. Sara looked ahead at the window opposite her and the scenery that was unfolding as the train sped past.

Five more stations and the train reached its terminus. Everyone made a beeline towards the exits. Natalie held of Sara's hand, which caught the latter momentarily off guard, but she thought maybe the old lady needed some support. Finally, when they had alighted, Sara glanced at Natalie to bid her good-bye, when the old lady tightened her hold on Sara's left forearm and said, "I want you to come home for a cup of coffee."

Sara protested and said she was already late and her aunt would be waiting, but Natalie would hear none of it. "You are my guest and I'll treat you as one, rest assured."

More protestations emanated from Sara, but Natalie's oft repeated two words, 'I insist', were difficult to be unheeded. So, reluctantly enough, Sara walked alongside Natalie, who stomped the ground with her walking stick, as she plodded her way towards her home.

Natalie's home was in a slightly wooded area abutting the railway line and it was here that the duo was now headed. Sara glanced at her watch and it told her that she was, indeed, running late. Poor Rachel, her aunt, would be waiting to have lunch with her.

After having walked for a good twenty minutes, Natalie's home appeared to come in sight. It was a cottage with a red-tiled roof surrounded by a few trees and a bed of flowers The entire precincts were bounded by a fencing of barbed wire and there was a wicket gate on one corner which had a drive-way beyond leading to the door of the cottage.

"Here, we are now," said Natalie, as she loosened the grip on Sara's forearm. "That's my house. Do you like it?"

"It's beautiful, and it's so peaceful around here."

Natalie stepped up and pressed the key into the lock.

"Do you live here, alone?" asked Sara, rather tepidly, this being probably the only question that she had asked of Natalie.

"No, my dear. My children stay along with me, but they may be resting or doing some job, and I don't wish to disturb them. That's why I always carry this key with me."

"Oh," gasped Sara, but the word hardly came out of her mouth.

Natalie gave a quick twist to the handle after inserting the key and stepped through the open door. "Come on in, come right in," she told a waiting Sara. The latter looked in and found the house quite dimly lit. Reluctantly, she put her right foot in and then lifted her left foot from the last step in front of the door. "Make yourself comfortable," said Natalie, motioning towards the opulent sofas. Sara cuddled up against a corner of a sofa more out of a feeling of trepidation than out of awe at the grandeur of the interiors.

"I'll be with you in a jiffy, with a steaming cup of the most delicious coffee," said Natalie with a chuckle.

As the old lady vanished from sight, headed presumably to the kitchen, Sara looked around the spacious drawing room which was well-appointed with artefacts from across the world and medallions and awards won over the years. There were beautiful paintings artistically laid out across the walls and expensive carpets covered the floor. A state-of-the-art chandelier adorned the ceiling and its crystals gleamed even in the dim light. For all the expensive goods within the room, Sara felt that the upkeep was wanting, as every piece of furniture had a layer of dust on it. Cobwebs gained ground on the ceiling and the carpet kicked up dust when it was stepped on. 'Why do the inmates of this house stay in this filth?' thought Sara.

She stood up as she heard footfalls approaching the room. A middle-aged woman entered and smiled at Sara. "So, you're the girl my mother was speaking about in the kitchen. Welcome to our house. She'll be with you, right away, with a cup of coffee. She's always been an expert at making coffee. With the right quantity of powder, milk and sugar, she's been a great asset to lift us out of boredom or fatigue."

"Could I make a call to my aunt, because she would be waiting for my arrival?" asked Sara, rather defensively.

"Oh, but the phone is dead, my dear, and the lineman has yet to repair it in spite of repeated reminders. Anyway, I'll tell my mother not to hold you up for long, but please come another day and spend some time with us."

"I sure will do that."

The lady left and Sara waited for her coffee to arrive. After about fifteen minutes and no sign of the coffee, Sara gingerly trooped out of the drawing room and tiptoed towards what seemed to be the kitchen. Everything seemed to be in a mess and there was no coffee brewing on the fire. Sara felt a little uncomfortable as she looked around for Natalie. There was no trace of her. Beyond the kitchen, Sara could see a room which was dark and looked ominous. Something told her she had better leave as soon as possible. Following her conscience, she stepped back into the drawing room and then went out of the main door. Even though she was bathed in the rays of the bright morning sun, Sara felt a trifle cold. For some unknown treason, a chill went down her spine. As she went down the small driveway, she thought she heard a cacophony of sounds coming from the direction of the house, as if several voices were talking together spiced with cynical laughter, She hurried through the wicket gate and, as she stepped onto the main road, a labourer who had seen her coming from the direction of the cottage, stood still and then took to his heels.

"That's strange," said Sara to herself. "Do I look weird?" Then with a shrug, she descended down an incline and made her way to a taxi stand from where she hired a taxi to her aunt's home.

Rachel, her aunt, was indeed waiting for her. "Whatever happened to you, my dear? Why are you late? Is everything okay? I was getting worried so I had called up your mother and she said you had left well in time to reach here for lunch. But it's two-o-clock now and that's the reason for my worry."

"Oh, everything is fine, aunty. I met an old lady in the train who stuck to me and insisted that I go to her place along with her. She offered to make me a cup of coffee and, much as I protested that I was already late, she wouldn't let me go and held me firmly on my left forearm, till she led me to her home."

"And how was the coffee?"

"I didn't have any." Sara, then, set about to narrate all that had transpired in the cottage.

At the end of it, her aunt exclaimed," You don't mean to say that you went to the cottage in a slightly wooded area about a couple of furlongs away from the station, do you?"

"Yes, that's it. That's where I went."

Rachel went pale in the face as she turned and looked squarely at Sara. "That cottage, my dear is uninhabited. It has been so for more than two years, ever since the entire family died in a shipwreck. People now say that the place is haunted."

On an impulse, Sara screamed and went and hugged her aunt. Later, she glanced at her left forearm. The marks of Natalie's finger nails still seemed to show up, albeit in a slightly faded manner.

THE END

5

R.I.P.

The grace of that face would never be lit again with her charming smile. An imposing personality, she was respected in the entire village and the news of her death was received with sorrow and disbelief. "Amma passed away in her sleep. The end came after a massive heart attack." Shobhana was explaining the sequence of events leading to the death of Sarla Rajasekharan, her mother and the matriarch of the family, to the village folk who had come trooping to the palatial ancestral home of Rajasekharan Namboodiri, after receiving the news of her death to have a last glimpse of their beloved *thampurati*. The vast hall on the ground floor of the mansion wore a gloomy look. The redeeming feature was the fragrance of incense sticks which pervaded across a wide area. From early morning, relatives of the aged lady had started arriving from far and near. She had touched the hearts of everyone who came in contact with her. Never failing the poor and needy, often her gentle touch on a child's head was enough to raise the latter from a spell of despondency. For the simple village people, she was a benevolent person who would mingle with them whenever it was possible and try and mitigate their difficulties. After the death of her husband several years earlier, her daughter and her family had left their home in another district and moved in to stay with her in the *tharavadu* or ancestral house. Her son, Vishnu, and his family were settled in the U.S.A., where he held an enviable position in a leading university.

As people filed past her body, which was encased in a temperature-controlled casket, word went round that the funeral rites and cremation would only take place after the arrival of Vishnu, possibly in a couple of days. Vishnu, who was obviously grief-stricken, had immediately started making preparations to leave for India at the earliest possible flight. He and his family arrived the next day, a little late into the night, and were received by Shobhana, her husband, Gopinathan, and their two children, Arya and Bhuvan. Vishnu's wife, Ambika, was raring to meet Shobhana, although the circumstances did not warrant a warm welcome. Their children, Ammini and Mohan were about the same age as Arya and Bhuvan and so got along very well together.

The following day, the priests arrived to conduct the last rites and then it was made known that the funeral would take place later in the day, culminating in the cremation before dusk. The funeral rites, prior to the body being taken for cremation, having been conducted, the body was taken in a truck bedecked with flowers and garlands with a large portrait of a smiling Sarla adorning the highest point of the truck, through the main thoroughfares of the village with the crowd ever surging in increasing numbers at every nook and junction, before it was laid on the funeral pyre and consigned to flames by a visibly distraught Vishnu, who had fleeting memories of his early childhood spent in the company of his parents, pass before his eyes every time a tongue of flame seemed to lick a log of sandalwood, before the mortal remains were consumed by the lit pyre. The cremation having been completed, the grieving family returned to their ancestral home to spend the night in solitude.

Early in the morning, the next day, Vishnu and Gopinathan left to collect the ashes in a clay urn from the cremation site and then the entire family left to immerse these in the holy waters. After completing certain other rituals, they returned to their house where they were met by a gentleman in an advocate's uniform who introduced himself as being Sarla's advocate, Sashidharan, who had heard the news of her demise but could not make it for the funeral as he was held up elsewhere in connection with a case. Vishnu and Gopinathan joined their palms in an impromptu *namaste* which was immediately reciprocated and then the two gentlemen led the advocate into the spacious hall of the opulent mansion. Chairs were laid out and the family sat down to hear what the advocate had in store for them.

At the outset, Sashidharan apologized for not having been present at the obsequies and then paid glowing tributes to the departed soul. He then made the purpose of his visit clear. "I have brought the will of Madam Sarla Rajasekharan, which had been entrusted to me about five years ago in a sealed cover. I had then been advised that I should arrive at this mansion post haste and reveal the contents of the same in the presence of the entire family of her two children, in the event of her demise. As I understand, her children and all the members of their families are here, are they not?" Sashidharan looked around at the small crowd to receive some confirmation.

"Yes, that's right," replied Vishnu, with a nod. "We're all here. You may proceed with your task."

Sashidharan took out the sealed envelope from his briefcase and held it before him for all to see. "As you may observe, this cover was sealed in the presence of madam. It has her signatures on the seals to authenticate this fact." So saying, he handed the cover to Vishnu for his verification and then it was passed on to the others. Fully satisfied with the veracity of the envelope, they handed it back to Sashidharan who cut one of its corners with a pair of scissors and then tore the side with a paper cutter. All heads waited expectantly to see what was to emerge. Sashidharan removed a single sheet of paper from within and held it above his shoulder. The family could see that it was a handwritten note with Sarla's signature appended below. "May I begin?" he asked.

"Yes, you may," prompted Vishnu.

"*This is to state that the following declaration may be treated as my last and final will,*" beganSashidharan, as he proceeded to read the will. He continued, "*All that which was passed on to me by my husband, Shri Rajasekharan Namboodiri, be it property, valuables, artefacts, furniture and furnishings or residual bank balances, shall be quantified and entered in a register, for the purposes of record and then an appropriate valuation done by persons in the know of such practices. This shall be arranged by my advocate, Shri Vadakkemaddathe Sashidharan and he shall ensure the satisfactory completion of this exercise. I have already discussed this aspect with him and he is in agreement of the same. For this task, he shall be paid an honorarium which shall be decided in consensus by my children. After the valuation is completed, the same may be divided into two equal parts, to be distributed among Vishnu and Shobhana. In the unforeseen event of either*" *or both of them predeceasing me, the equal parts shall devolve to the respective families. The wealth may be distributed in kind in the present condition of the various assets or after being liquidated in monetary terms. I leave it to the judgement of my children as to how they wish to proceed in this matter. I am sure that there will not be any confusion or misunderstanding in the execution of this will and I will rely on advocate Sashidharan to ensure that there is a smooth transition of my wealth to my children."* Sashidharan looked up from the paper and surveyed the family before him. It was clear that everyone had comprehended the simple and straightforward will. *"However,"* he said, as he continued to read the will, *"my children would need to comply with a condition that I wish to impose. After the quantification and valuation of the wealth has been undertaken and satisfactorily completed, they and their families would need to reside in the ancestral home for a continuous period of not less than one month. I have to insist on this on account of the fact that there is an age-old superstition in our family which states that if the owner of the ancestral house dies while residing in it, his or her soul will not get salvation should the house be deserted thereafter or disposed off without the descendants having stayed in it for a period not less than one month."*

"That's about it," remarked Sashidharan, as he addressed the gathering. "I'll get in touch with you, once I have been able to arrange for the requisite wealth assessors. If you have any questions, you may ask me now."

"Currently, I will not be able to stay in India beyond a couple of days, as I have to resume my employment as soon as possible," said Vishnu. "Consequently, my stay in this house along with my family would have to be relegated for about two years from now. I would, nevertheless, rely on the oversight of my sister Shobhana and her husband,

Gopinathan, in the whole matter regarding the valuation of the wealth. My family shall also remain in India to provide for any assistance till the valuation has been completed. Besides, with regard to the wealth being distributed in kind or in monetary terms, my wife and I would like to discuss the matter in private with Shobhana and Gopinathan, for which purpose, we shall move to an adjacent room. Hopefully, it would not take much time, for which I request you to bear with us."

"Please take your time. I can wait," replied Sashidharan, with a smile.

So, Vishnu and Shobhana along with their spouses excused themselves and had a detailed discussion on the distribution of wealth. Gopinathan's job in a local bank earned him a moderate salary. His middle-class background and present lifestyle goaded him to urge Shobhana to call for the liquidation of the wealth. The latter was game for this as she did not have any presumptions of continuing to stay in the humongous house with a team of house helps to maintain it. She also preferred receiving her dues in cash. This was communicated to Vishnu and Ambika, who reciprocated her sentiments. The four also discussed regarding the honorarium to be paid to Sashidharan and agreed on a figure of five lakh rupees. With a consensus decision having been arrived at, the four trooped back to the main hall where Sashidharan and their kids were patiently waiting for them.

"We would wish to have the entire wealth to be liquidated and settled equally between me and my sister," averred Vishnu.

Sashidharan nodded in comprehension.

"Besides," continued Vishnu, "Would an honorarium of five lakh rupees be acceptable to you?"

"Thank you. I accept your offer," said Sashidharan, with his right palm going instinctively to his chest.

"So, it is now decided that you will complete the quantification, valuation and sale of all the property and items in the precincts of this house and, together with the cash and bank balances, would arrive at a figure which would form the basis of distribution. For this purpose, you would engage wealth assessors, auctioneers and others in the know of disposal of the items, such that you would receive, in the best of your knowledge and belief, the most attractive price for each asset. The services of such external agents would be paid for from the amount finally arrived at after liquidation of assets or prior to that, as the case may be. To place the rudiments of this task on record, I would request you to draft an agreement between you and me and my sister, which would seal the deal that now exists between us in our verbal understanding." Vishnu paused to drink a glass of water.

"Absolutely, you have said everything that I had intended to say," remarked Sashidharan. "I shall send across two copies of the will in a sealed cover for your information and record, while I retain the original till the final distribution of wealth in monetary terms. Thereafter, I shall be absolved of all responsibilities relating to the will."

"Perfect," said Vishnu. "We shall wait to hear from you."

"If there is nothing else to be discussed, may I now take leave of you?"

"Yes, you may. There is nothing more for the present to be discussed."

"Thank you, all. It was a privilege to meet you, although it had to be in such tragic circumstances." So saying, Sashidharan picked up his briefcase and made his way through the door.

After seeing him off, the two families gathered together for partaking of a sparse meal. Vishnu left in a couple of days, leaving his family behind as decided earlier. The sixteenth day ceremony was organized by Gopinathan, Shobhana and Ambika where a large number of relatives, friends and village folk congregated to savour the generous *sadhya* or feast. Thereafter, there was nothing much to do except wait for some action to be generated from the side of the advocate. So, the three adults decided on locking up the house with all its contents and then returned to their respective homes which they had bought in the heart of Cochin.

Rajasekharan Namboodiri's father, Vishwanathan Namboodiri was the collector of the district during his long tenure in the Indian Administrative Service, after which he went on to hold more senior and influential positions. A dominant personality, he held his sway among the political clout, and was respected for his supposedly forthright and tactful decisions. For many, he was the paragon for emulation, in their dreams to enter the threshold of government service. He was also from a wealthy family and, being the only son of his parents, had inherited from both sides, considerable amount of wealth in terms of jewellery and valuables, artefacts and curios and several other rare items. After his demise, the entire wealth passed on to Rajasekharan Namboodiri, as the latter's sibling, Gangadharan Namboodiri, who was a bachelor, had predeceased his father.

Now, one cannot please everyone in this world. Even when a person does good things and takes tough decisions, he is sure to step on someone else's shoes. So also was the case with Vishwanathan Namboodiri. His straightforward approach and attitude, no doubt won him plaudits, but also earned him the wrath of the land and mining mafia. Their nefarious activities had been crushed by the courage and bold decisions of Vishwanathan Namboodiri and they had been sorely licking their wounds over the years. Just like the exploits and good deeds of the family's patriarch was narrated and retold during his generation and in subsequent generations, so also the wounds that he had inflicted on the mafia were carefully nurtured with a spirit of vengeance and retribution during that generation and in subsequent generations. So currently, there were grandchildren of the mafia lords baying for revenge at the first opportunity that was available to them.

Therefore, it was not surprising that they soon got wind of the tragedy in the family and the fact that the ancestral home was temporarily shut till the valuation of the assets was to take place. In this scenario, it was very convenient for them to inflict some damage without any suspicion.

Located on top of a hill, the ancestral home commanded a majestic view of the countryside below. The home's spacious precincts displayed a variety of flora as well as a number of fruit and coconut trees. Even from the foothills, the view of the house was pristine and beautiful. However, in the absence of the folk who had stayed there, it now wore a deserted look, as the villagers, too, had no occasion to amble up for seeking a solution for any grievance.

The descendants of the mafia, therefore, hatched a plan. They would climb the steps on the hill on a new moon night when the night would be pitch dark and with great precision and stealth, set the entire mansion and its wooded precincts ablaze. For this, they needed to assemble the materials that were required for the purpose which they went about garnering with tremendous zeal. The night of the new moon was four days hence and they decided that the deed would be executed on that very night.

True to their sinister design, the palatial mansion and its precincts went up in flames as the evil-doers sprayed fuel and torched it from all possible angles. In the enveloping darkness, they made good their escape and soon joined the multitude of dumbfounded and bewildered villagers who beheld the conflagration from a safe distance away from the foothills. The heavy woodwork in the ancestral home as well as the surrounding trees facilitated the sustenance and spread of the fire and by the time the fire brigade personnel arrived, about forty five minutes after they were informed of the fire, the *tharavadu* house of the Namboodiris was almost reduce to a rubble. The flames were eventually extinguished but nothing remained to tell the story of the majestic mansion that had once stood out as an imposing landmark.

The police arrived and encircled the area to prevent trespassers from interfering with any clues that may have been material to solve the case. From their preliminary investigation, it was apparent to them that this was a clear case of arson. But, in the absence of any witness and a motive for the crime, the police could not make any headway in the case, even after a couple of years, and they decided to treat it as a case on hold for the time being, for want of evidence.

When the family was informed on the day following the incident, they were horrified and rushed to the location only to find ashes and rubble lying on the land that now harboured the ruins of their ancestral home, its contents and the precincts. Everyone was reduced to tears at the terrible sight but there nothing one could do. On the advice of the police, they remained at the site to try and salvage, with some external help from the villagers, such items like gold used for ornaments which would not have been destroyed by the fire. On a careful scrutiny, they were able to retrieve whatever gold was visible, but beyond that everything else was of no value. They informed Vishnu of the new tragedy and he came down to India post haste to take stock and decide on the next course of action. But try as he might to obtain some relevant information from the villagers, his efforts were fruitless as the villains had absconded without a trace. So he filed a complaint with the police of an act of arson against 'unknown persons'. The advocate was also informed accordingly and he promised to follow up on the case as it unfolded.

For Sukumar, Rajesh and Veerabhadran, the descendants of the mafia, it was a time for enjoyment. They got together and wined and dined in expensive hotels to savour their ill-gotten pleasure to its fullest extent. They were all staying far away in another district and there was no way that the law would have had any clue of their involvement in the crime. And this, in fact, was true for they did not have a care in the world as they went about their lives without any hitch, or so it seemed.

It was nearing festival time, for *onam*, or the harvest festival, was not far away. Sukumar's family had been urging him to take them on an excursion to a nearby hill, where the air was very pure and there was a wide view available of the surrounding habitation. Now, with a renewed zeal for life, Sukumar agreed to the proposal with a suddenness that took his wife by surprise. So, on a weekend, the family along with some relatives packed their bags and carried some tents and ample amount of foodstuff and set out towards their destination for an overnight stay, even as Sukumar's wife remarked prior to leaving that it was a day where the night would be very dark on account of a new moon. Sukumar shrugged the comment as being fraught with negativity and asked her to think no more about it.

The party arrived at the foothills in good time when the sun was still in the east. The climb was not arduous as they went through well-defined pathways and soon the picnic party had reached the top from where the view of the countryside below was spectacular. Plastic and cloth mats were spread out with a few pillows thrown in and the crowd settled down to have an early lunch. The children then decided to play badminton while some of the adults settled down for a game of cards. Others went about on an exploring spree while yet a couple of men were involved in a game of chess. Tea was served around 4.00 p.m. and then everyone agreed for a walk on the flattened piece of the hill that made up the summit. The sun had begun to set in the horizon and Sukumar and the other men prepared to face the darkness that was to descend upon them. They delved into their knapsacks to take out torches and battery-operated lanterns and equipped their women-folk with these lighting equipments accordingly. Tents were erected and thereafter, the men got involved in a serious discussion on the state's politics with an occasional digression into the state of the traffic infrastructure. There were other topics too, on which the assemblage found interest in spending their time while the women were busy with their gossip, sharing notes on recipes and narrating stories of movies they had seen. The children had a rollicking time playing 'passing the parcel' and singing songs. At around 8.00 p.m. there was the announcement of dinner and everyone huddled around a small campfire which had been lit with a few logs retrieved from the periphery of the summit. With a pleasant breeze blowing and the sounds of crickets coupled with the sparkle of an occasional firefly setting the ambience of a perfect outdoor gathering, the small crowd relished the array of dishes which were doled out in sumptuous quantities. The men then moved away for a smoke and continuation of the discussion on miscellaneous topics which had been cut short by the announcement of dinner. About an hour later, it was time to turn in for the night and the women-folk and children occupied most of the tents while a couple was reserved only for men. The men did not sleep immediately but, seating themselves around in a circle within a tent, indulged in a quiet session of consuming 'small' pegs of liquor repacked in a mineral water bottle which they had assiduously kept out of range of the women and children. When this brief session of sporadic entertainment ended, drowsiness overcame the motley crowd and they stretched out on the laid-out mats and dozed off, all except Sukumar. He was wide awake as if energized by the drink. After a while, feeling a little bored and not getting sleep, he picked up his torch and decided to take a stroll. He walked around the perimeter of the summit, savouring the beautiful sight of dotted lights dressing up the landscape at the foothills below. He must have walked for about ten minutes or so and now he came to stand beside a rock that jutted out from the side of the hill.

As he stood there for a few moments, he heard a sound behind him. It was a chuckle of an elderly person. Where could it have come from? There was no one else on the summit except he and his friends. He looked behind him and all around – there was nobody in sight. Maybe he must have imagined it. The peg of liquor must be taking its toll. He turned around to have a final look at the countryside below and then he heard it again. This time he was sure that someone had chuckled. He was not dreaming. With a quick reflex action, he turned all round and then he saw her. It was a sinister sight of an old lady, clad in white with deep-set eyes and a sadistic smile crossing her chapped lips. She was trudging towards him and now was only a few feet away. Sukumar froze to the ground below him which seemed to be giving way. He tried to bolt but couldn't, so consumed was he with fear. He developed goose-pimples instantaneously and a chill went down his spine.

"*Ayyo*, she's coming to kill me." Sukumar gave a full-throttled cry. This woke up a couple of men, who woke up the others in the tent to find out what was happening. They all emerged with their torches and went in the direction of the sound. They could now see Sukumar standing on the edge of the hill, seemingly involved in a wrestling bout with some imaginary object. He happened to see them, for he again shouted, "Help, she's trying to kill me." The men advanced quickly towards him, but all they could see was a frightened Sukumar gesticulating violently, trying to ward off some invisible force.

"Who is it? We don't see anybody," ventured one amongst the lot of bewildered men. There was no reply from Sukumar. He was now furiously fighting off an unseen and presumably violent adversary with all his might. But it seemed to be a losing battle, for every moment he was pushed backwards towards the very edge of the hill. One of the men ran forward to pull Sukumar away from the precipice, but was thrown backwards as if struck by some brute force. Sukumar now stood on the very brink and then before everyone's eyes, he tilted and was gone. After hitting the piece of jutting rock, his body had a free fall all the way to the bottom of the foothills. The men were aghast. A terrified look passed from one to the other like the baton in a relay race and with careful steps they advanced towards the edge. They looked down but could not see the body in the darkness.

By this time, some women had also woken up and were running towards the men. The latter explained what they had seen. There was a hue and cry as Sukumar's wife and then his children burst out in tears and were inconsolable; but for those who had seen and heard the episode, it was a foreboding mystery. The group packed their belongings and at the first sight of dawn, began their descent. They went over to the other side of the hill and located the body which was smashed beyond recognition. The police were informed and they arrived and began their investigation.

Ignorant of the tragedy that had befallen his associate, Veerabhadran was making all the preparations for a grand *onam* or harvest festival. He had invited quite a few of his friends and relatives and their families for the ceremonies and the grand *sadhya*. Finally, the day of *thiruonam* dawned and the guests started trooping in. A large *pandal* or temporary structure with canopy was erected and chairs and tables were laid out in the large courtyard. A festive mood descended as children ran about and played in gay abandon. The adults got introduced to one another and soon a lot of bonhomie was built up in an around Veerabhadran's house. It was clear that a rush of positive energy had begun to surge everywhere.

It was time for lunch and the sumptuous *sadhya* was being served in plantain leaves as the guests sat on either side of long tables and enjoyed the multi-course meal. A few rounds of this serving continued as the guests could not all be seated together at the same time. The elaborate repast over, the guests retracted into small clusters in the courtyard and within the house to dwell on topics that interested them as also to share news about their families and neighbourhoods.

The afternoon was well spent and a game of cards and other board games went underway as the women-folk were engrossed watching a movie on TV. Soon, tea, coffee and delicious snacks were served by the house helps which were lapped up with great fervour. As the evening rays of the sun caused the shadows to lengthen, Veerabhadran announced there would be a grand display of fireworks after sundown. There was heightened enthusiasm as everyone eagerly waited for the light and sound spectacle to commence.

At around 8.00 p.m. the first 'rocket' soared into the atmosphere. From a respectable height, it sprayed a shower of ignited chemicals which represented the picture of an umbrella. This was followed up with the 'launch' of multiple 'rockets', each conveying a different picture of its shower. The display of 'rocket' fire was interspersed with the bursting of crackers tied together in clusters. Along came the sparklers which were a real hit amongst the children. They rotated these lit metal sticks coated with chemicals, in vertical circles to project a brilliant spectacle to the viewers.

Veerabhadran's brother, Krishnan, had decided to burst the 'elephant crackers' towards the end of the fireworks display. These were so called, on account of the tremendous blast each produced. Each of these looked like a wrapped-up chocolate cube with a wick protruding from a corner. It was now nearing the end and so he brought out his stock and the blasts commenced. Four such crackers had the audience clasp their ears to restrict the sound but yet, everyone seemed to revel in the extravaganza.

Krishnan lit the fifth cracker and instinctively moved away. But the almost instantaneous bang didn't happen. He waited and then with measured steps moved forward to investigate.

"Stop," cried Veerabhadran. "I'll see what the problem is." He moved forward, as the crowd which had now swelled with people arriving from nearby areas, waited with bated breath. "The wick is not lit," he announced. A matchbox was handed over to him and he prepared to light the cracker, yet another time. As his hand with the lit matchstick moved towards the wick, the latter caught fire in an apparent case of late ignition after it had been ignited the first time by Krishnan. Veerabhadran, being in close proximity, received the full force of the blast on his face and chest. He fell down with his clothes on fire. Someone ran into the house and brought a bucket of water which was used to douse the flames that had begun to envelope the upper portion of his body. A shocked audience held their breath. The fireworks display was over.

Soon an ambulance pulled up and took Veerabhadran to the hospital. The doctors confirmed he had lost his eyesight and had suffered forty percent burns in the critical parts of his body. They battled to save his life in the ICU but after a few hours, Veerabhadran breathed his last.

A few months later, at the height of winter, Rajesh was driving towards a hill resort in Wayanad to meet one of his college friends who had announced his arrival on vacation. It was well into the evening with the weather being foggy and visibility rather poor. The incline was not steep and so Rajesh placed his foot on the accelerator and drove at a comfortable pace. After about ten minutes of driving, he was encountering a bend when, even in the dimly lit road, he saw an old lady dressed in white staring at him from the wayside, in the middle of nowhere. He found it odd that the lady was standing at a place where there were no houses nearby. He wanted to stop and offer her a lift but the speed at which he was travelling had already taken him round the bend. His mind having been distracted at the sight of the lady, he was unable to control the car as it turned the corner. And there at the bend was propped up on a jack, almost in the middle of the road, a stationary truck carrying some construction material. Before he knew what was happening, Rajesh had driven right onto the truck. Such was the impact that the car burst into flames. Rajesh was hurt but still alive. He struggled to open the door of car but apparently it was jammed. He tried the other doors but these were also jammed. As the flames spread throughout the car, he looked on hopefully for some help, but no one was in sight. The fire soon engulfed the car and very soon, he was in flames, having gone through the ordeal of seeing death in the face.

Meanwhile, a grieving family followed up with the police for any news regarding progress in the case of arson of their ancestral home, but to no avail. Little did they know that the punishment for the miscreants which was to have justly come from the legal system was quietly woven and executed in a trail of retribution by the restless spirit of Sarla Rajasekharan.

Vishnu returned from the USA after his retirement and constructed an imposing bungalow on the same land where his ancestral home once stood. He and his family along with Shobhana and her family stepped into the house with full confidence that their stay for one month or more would bring peace to their mother's soul.

And so, indeed, Sarla Rajasekharan's soul was witness to a satisfactory end to the sordid tale of events. As her wish in her will finally found its fulfillment, her portrait in the hallway radiated with charm and composure, and it seemed to say, "Thank you, my children, you have made my day. I can now rest in peace."

THE END

<u>GLOSSARY</u>

1.*Thampurati*: A female ruler, noblewoman, or queen

2.*Tharavadu*: Ancestral home or family house

3.*Namaste*: respectfully offering salutation by joining the palms and saying 'namaskar'

4.*Sadhya*: an opulent lunch or feast normally served on plantain leaves on ceremonial occasions

5.*Pandal*: a temporary shelter erected normally with bamboo poles to support a canopy as a roof

6.*Onam*: harvest festival in Kerala

7.*Thiruonam*: the most auspicious day of the Onam festival

6
Shadow Of Vengeance

The landscape of Bangalore, or Bengaluru as it is known now, was changing. The computer revolution had converted the city, India's Silicon Valley, into a hub of construction activity. Gone were the days when locals would laze on the porch in front of their individual houses, taking in the fresh air and vibrant fragrances of the abundant flora catching one's eye along neat promenades at every nook and corner of the laid back city. Now, the very identity of the metropolis was undergoing a metamorphosis – for, all of a sudden, tall skyscrapers had begun to dot the skyline of this beautiful city with its well-known salubrious weather and myriads of gardens and parks. Everything was now being geared up to welcome the advent of the computer age in this rather sleepy city.

The boom in the construction activity brought in its wake a migration of a large number of the working class population, mostly daily wage labourers from far-flung places of the huge nation. They came to the city in hordes with willing hands and an awe-struck vision of transforming their impoverished lives into a destiny of promise. Work was now being made available, plenty of it, as the business of accommodating the transient and permanent white collar employees and senior executives, many of them from abroad, got underway at a fast pace.

Among the labourers who travelled to Bangalore was Birju, a thirty-year-old landless cultivator, from distant Bihar who traversed the journey on foot and in an unreserved compartment of a locomotive. With hardly any savings from his meagre wages as a cultivator, he had decided to try his luck in the construction industry, for he believed that the returns from developing real estate would be amply more than that of agriculture and he would be a consequent beneficiary in this prosperous business. So leaving behind his ageing parents and three children in the care of his wife, he landed in the city to begin a new chapter in his life and his fortunes.

Birju had nowhere to go in particular. He did not know anyone in Bangalore and there was no one waiting with open arms to receive him. He had no job opening that he could access immediately on arrival and so for a couple of days he eked out an existence with a few rupees which he had assiduously rolled up and tied in a knot in the folds of his *dhoti*. At night, he found shelter in one of the sections of a water pipe lying scattered by the wayside. On the third day, after persistent follow-up with the supervisor at a building construction site, he was absorbed as a 'grade C' labourer which reflected his inadequacies in skill for the task in question. Nevertheless, Birju decided to accept the job even though it meant that his income was less than his previous one.

He was a sincere worker and accomplished all the menial tasks that were piled up on him without as much as a murmur. He was an eager learner also and had the hunger in his belly to grasp the intricacies of certain tasks which were assigned to him from time to time. Soon, he got the admiration of his supervisor for his sincerity and willingness to accept and complete every task that was handed over to him. In due course, therefore, he rose in the ranks to be a semi-skilled worker in 'grade B'.

Birju's supervisor, Malpani, was not a hard task master but he had a knack of motivating his staff and ensuring the construction activity was on track for he was always pursuing seemingly lost causes of his subordinates with the developer, Mahesh Rathi, to try and find solutions to their multifarious problems. Sometimes he succeeded and on many other occasions his efforts bore no fruits. For his initiatives to mitigate the suffering of the labourers, the latter held him in high esteem and did everything as per his bidding.

It was now about three years that Birju was in the job. During this time, he had not seen his family and now he wished to take some unpaid leave and visit his folks. He approached Malpani with his request and was granted fifteen days to travel to his native village and be with his kin. Malpani had a soft corner for Birju on account of the latter's devotion to his duty. Birju was overjoyed. He immediately set about making a few purchases of clothes for everyone at home and a couple of wooden dolls for his four-year-old child from the measly savings he had carefully garnered, being residual earnings after having sent regular dispatches of money orders to his family over the three years. Everything was packed into a cloth bundle and tied to the end of a stout stick. He was now ready for his trip and, after bidding farewell to Malpani and his colleagues, he set about on his journey.

He reached his village late in the evening, the following day, and was overwhelmed by the spontaneity of love and affection that was showered on him. His family was well and had pulled on with his remittances and his wife had even taken up some stitching assignments to augment the family income. He had a lot to tell them and after all the initial euphoria of seeing each other waned, he basked in the bright sunshine and pristine air surrounding his hovel playing with his children or giving his parents a massage of their legs and hands. It was a welcome change for him from the dust and grime surrounding the building construction in Bangalore. However, the fifteen days that he had flew past even before he had begun to settle down to appreciate the concerns of his family. He wished he could stay on a little longer but he had promised Malpani that he would return as scheduled; and so, with a heavy heart he kissed his folks good bye before departing at the break of dawn, the following day.

Malpani was pleased with Birju's integrity and commitment to work and welcomed him on his arrival. He had initiated a change in the job profile for Birju, which he thought would help him in his career progression. And so, from a mason laying bricks the whole day long, Birju was now assigned the job of a painter. He worked as an apprentice initially, learning the ropes from the established worker in the job and then took upon the responsibility to complete several interior and exterior painting jobs with finesse.

It was the beginning of June and Bangalore was experiencing heavy rainfall at the start of the monsoon season. In such inclement weather, the construction activity was kept in abeyance till the situation improved. So the labourers, including Birju, had a couple of days of rest and when the rainfall subsided, they once again returned to their assigned tasks. Birju was currently painting the exterior of the building. Perched high above the ground on bamboo scaffolding, he dipped his brush into the thick paint kept in a bucket which hung from the scaffolding a feet away from him and then applied it evenly in few quick strokes. This building which was a high rise of twenty floors was the developer's signature project and everything needed to be done right. The developer, incidentally, had booked the entire penthouse with a self-contained swimming pool for himself and his family of wife and a kid. As Birju applied smart strokes with the paint brush, he hummed a tune from a popular Bollywood movie. A stiff breeze blew across and made Birju feel a trifle cold, but he was now used to these sudden changes in the Bangalore weather and he continued with his swishing and swashing of the paint brush.

Occasionally, he would glance at the traffic on the road below where the cars would appear as miniature models. He had overcome his fear of heights ever since he had taken up his new assignment and now he was at home with his paint and brush working with confidence from a position which would have made any layman dizzy to the core. He thought of his family as he applied paint to a pillar on the exterior of the building. They had all felt despondent at the time of his departure and after wishing him well, hoped he would return soon. He felt nostalgic and reached for his wallet in his pant pocket where he had tucked away the family photograph in its folds. He looked at the photograph and a tear welled up in his eye. He wiped it off with the sleeve of his shirt and deposited the wallet in the inmost recesses of his pant pocket. He continued with quick strokes of the brush but his heart was heavy and his concentration had waned.

As he moved alongside the scaffolding, his leg hit a stump and slipped on the bamboo pole causing his leg to give away. This had a domino effect on him as he tried to retain his grasp on the scaffolding, but the gap was too wide and in the unfortunate uncertainty which followed, he fell through the gap and hit a portion of the scaffolding below. His wails could be heard as he hurtled towards the parking lot. In no time, his body landed on the ground with a loud thud. Some witnesses to the horrific tragedy came running towards the spot where Birju's body lay in a pool of blood. His face, or whatever was left of it, was contorted in a traumatic grimace as of one having been in the know of certain death. He had fallen from a height of about a hundred feet without the support of a harness or the guarantee of a safety net. As if by sheer coincidence, a group of pigeons feeding on some grain outside Birju's hut in his village took flight and was gone. His mother watched the phenomenon and shuddered from some unknown danger.

Malpani and the other workers were now at the spot where Birju had fallen and were waiting for the ambulance to arrive. At the hospital, the last hope that anyone might have harboured was nipped when the doctor on duty announced that the body was brought dead on arrival. Birju was gone and so were the dreams of his family of six, totally dependent on him. A pall of gloom hung over the motley group of labourers who had waited outside the hospital for some redeeming news from Malpani, but that was not to be.

After the body was finally handed over, Malpani informed Birju's wife and the latter was overcome with grief. Nevertheless, she summoned courage and, with her children and in-laws, arrived the following day for the last rites. It was an extremely pathetic sight of a family being made to grieve and grope in the dark without any imminent wherewithal to sustain their existence. Malpani and his labourers contributed what they could afford but there was no lumpsum compensation from the developer, Mahesh Rathi. In fact, he had not even turned up to meet the family of the deceased and offer his condolence.

The hospital had informed the police of the tragedy and it was being treated as a medico-legal case. A case of negligence on the part of the developer was filed which made Mahesh Rathi rush to his lawyer to apply for anticipatory bail. After the legal wrangles which took place in due course, Mahesh Rathi emerged unscathed with a fine of Rs.5000/- being levied on him with absolutely no jail term. Justice had been denied to Birju's family and everyone in the know of the case acknowledged this fact.

The dust having settled, Malpani made a fervent attempt with Mahesh Rathi to try and glean some decent lump sum amount as a financial help for Birju's family; but it was thwarted by the developer at the very instance the matter was broached to him. In fact, he was furious that Malpani was showing so much concern in the matter when even the court had given its verdict. The latter saw the writing on the wall and withdrew from making any further representation.

Six months went by. The building was now ready for occupation and all the owners of various apartments moved in. Mahesh Rathi, his wife, Jyotsna, and his twelve-year-old son, Nirmal, also took up residence in the penthouse in due course. With a whole floor at their disposal, it was a fabulous life that they looked forward to. The swimming pool had gleaming blue tiles which provided a semblance of the pristine blue ocean.

Mahesh Rathi thought it was a good idea to hold a grand house-warming party and so called all his relatives, friends and acquaintances for the gathering. There was plenty of wine and food and everyone had their fill and then departed after giving their best wishes to Mahesh and family for a pleasurable stay in their new abode.

Everything seemed to be fine for the family of three. Their sprawling apartment was admired by one and all as weeks and months passed by with occasional parties and gatherings. Mahesh's reputation as a developer par excellence gained ground in real estate circles and he was emboldened to undertake many other projects around the city of Bangalore.

That was the time when something peculiar seemed to occur one night when the three were fast asleep. It was Mahesh who heard the sound of footfalls caused by the squeak presumably of slippers in the open terrace garden outside the bedroom. He was up in a jiffy and with torch in hand he went outdoors to investigate the unusual occurrence. As he flashed the torch over a wide area, he did not see the presence of any intruder. Perplexed, he resigned to the thought that he must have dreamt the whole episode and was about to turn indoors, when he happened to glance at the far end of the terrace only to see the receding silhouette of a figure going right over the brink. Mahesh rubbed his eyes to make sure that he was not dreaming. No, it was true that he had indeed seen someone in the terrace.

"Who goes there?" Mahesh attempted a hoarse cry, partly out of anger and the rest out of fear.

There was no response. Mahesh ran towards the spot where he had seen the figure go over. He looked down but there was no evidence of anyone having fallen below. He was now visibly disturbed. What was it, man or beast that he had seen slip over the wall of the terrace? He had no answer.

Mahesh returned to his bedroom but he could not get sleep thereafter. He tossed and turned till the first rays of dawn shone through the fine strands of the blinds. He sat up in bed and then once again went to the spot where he had seen the figure disappear. There was nothing amiss, no evidence of anything untoward that had occurred. Still quite dazed, he went for a wash and then got ready to go for work. He was deep in thought and his silence was only broken by an occasional 'yes' or 'no' to the several questions that were posed to him by Jyotsna whom he did not want to be privy to the weird happenings of the previous night.

At work, he could not concentrate as the image of a figure disappearing over the terrace wall kept impinging on his mind, time and again. As he thought more about the incident, he decided to keep security guards round the clock outside his main door. Probably, that would help to ward off unpleasant visitors.

With the passage of time, Mahesh soon forgot about the incident as he dumped it into the realm of the subconscious. Jyotsna's initial perceptions of a change in the temperament of Mahesh were washed away in the tide of exuberance exuded by Mahesh over his recent successful projects. Life was once again worth living.

It was about six months since the time Mahesh had witnessed the nocturnal incident. He and Jyotsna were lounging by their poolside, with some snacks laid out and talking of nothing much in particular. Nirmal was trying out different strokes in the swimming pool with a great deal of *elan*. In between their conversation, Mahesh and Jyotsna eyed him idly as he tried to demonstrate his prowess in the water.

All of a sudden, Nirmal let out a cry. "Help, help, someone is trying to pull me down."

Mahesh jumped up from his comfortable seating position, took a step forward and then dived into the pool in full attire. As he swam towards his son the latter seemed to be going further away from him. He could see his son struggling against some unseen force with all his might as he splashed his hands in wild strokes to stay afloat. But the force, or whatever it was, literally was drawing him towards the far corner and deepest point of the pool.

Mahesh finally reached his son and tried to hold him by the waist but was jolted by a tremendous backlash that came as a bolt from the blue. The blow dazed him and threw him off guard and while he was still groping with the thought as to what hit him, he saw his son go under and then there was a series of bubbles which subsided in due course.

The fact that his son had drowned now dawned on him. He swam towards the spot where Nirmal went down and could now see his body at the bottom of the pool. Jyotsna, who all the while was witnessing the unfolding episode, gave a shriek when she saw Nirmal's body disappear under water. "Do something, oh do something," she shouted, hoping Mahesh would be able to rescue her son. Little did she know what had transpired in the pool was beyond human intervention.

Mahesh got out of the pool and in a measured tone announced to his dazed wife, "He's gone, Jyotsna, we've lost him."

"What are you saying?" responded a frenzied Jyotsna, clutching Mahesh's shirt with both hands and giving him a thorough shake.

"You heard me, he's gone. Our Nirmal is no more," cried out Mahesh, cupping his face with his hands and letting out a loud sob followed by violent shuddering.

Jyotsna let out a wail which rang out in the cool ambience of the descending twilight. She ran into the house and jumped onto her bed, all the while screaming and sobbing loudly. Mahesh followed her and tried to console her but she kept repeating, "Why couldn't you save him?"

"I tried, my dear, but my attempt was futile." He dared not tell her what he had experienced.

The police were informed and they registered a case of unnatural death. After the post mortem report confirmed that death was caused due to drowning, Mahesh and Jyotsna were cleared of all probable charges.

Mahesh was convinced that some evil had befallen his family. He did not share his suspicion with Jyotsna lest she get delirious over the issue. She was now gradually coming to terms with the loss and it would be unwise to rewind the clock, he thought.

However, when sufficient time had elapsed, he availed the services of a *pandit* who, having been apprised in secrecy of the issues in question, conducted elaborate prayers and other rites to ward off evil influences from intruding in the lives of Mahesh and Jyotsna.

Mahesh was now reassured that the sinister incidents of the past few months were part of a bygone phase in his and Jyotsna's life and they had nothing to fear in the days ahead. His presumptions appeared to be correct as both of them once again picked up the threads and moved on in life, although the birth and death anniversaries of their son did remind them periodically of his loss. Everything was moving back to the good old days where partying and gatherings held sway in their social interaction. People did express their sympathies at the loss the family had suffered but Mahesh was quick to acknowledge and digress into another topic of discussion. Meanwhile, think as much as he would, he still couldn't afford an explanation to the mysterious force that had knocked him off his balance in the pool.

Jyotsna had house helps for the most part of the day who would perform multifarious duties, besides a cook who left the house only after 8.00 p.m. once dinner was served. Jyotsna, was an exponent of Bharat Natyam, a classical form of Indian dance, as well as a painter. She used to indulge in these pursuits whenever she was inclined and at other times read books or did some embroidery.

It was the beginning of summer. About three months of warm weather would follow after the relatively cold winter months. Jyotsna had just finished her practice session of Bharat Natyam and was a trifle tired. She had a wash and then curled up on the couch with a novel. Over time, she became drowsy and the book fell of her hands and on to the floor. Sleep had overtaken her and she unknowingly had succumbed to it.

She was abruptly awakened by a slow, blood-curdling sound that seemed to penetrate her eardrums with the ease of a knife slicing through a block of cheese. For a moment, she looked around the room in a stupor. Did she actually hear something or was it in some dream? She stood up in an instant and saw a house help passing by in the corridor.

"Did you hear any strange sound just a short while ago, Kanta?" she asked.

"No madam, none at all."

"Strange, I can vouch that I heard something," persisted Jyotsna.

She moved a few paces to her right and was about to open the sliding glass door leading to the garden when the sound manifested itself again. There was no mistaking it now – it came from the remote corner of the room. What could it be? Had a dog or some other animal intruded into the house? She took measured steps as she moved stealthily towards the corner.

And then it happened. Hardly had she reached the spot from where the sound seemed to originate, when she was intercepted by a steady trickle, drop by drop, of a red liquid which seemed to fall from the ceiling. One of the drops fell on the tip of her nose and she instinctively wiped it with the palm of her hand. She glanced at it and then looked hard at it – blood it was, there was no mistaking it.

"Aaaaaaaaaaaah," she screamed loudly, and turned around to run away from the room. The moment she did that she was confronted with the most frightening spectacle of the apparition of a man, visible only waist upwards, with blood-shot eyes and teeth gnashing against a backdrop of an unearthly sound, emanating as it seemed from bowels of that ghastly creature.

Jyotsna let out another loud scream, then swooned and fell full length on the floor. Before her back hit the hard surface, her head struck the side of the wooden cot with some force and she lay on the floor unconscious and bleeding from the head.

The two loud screams from Jyotsna brought a couple of house helps running to her room. They were aghast to see her in the manner that she was lying on the floor and immediately rushed to the telephone to call Mahesh.

Now Mahesh was on a business trip overseas and had left only the previous day, and was currently not able to attend the phone possibly because of the difference in time zones. So the house helps decided to call the nearest hospital and arrange for an ambulance. The ambulance took about half-an-hour to reach and Jyotsna was shifted to the ICU. The doctors in attendance diagnosed her condition after a series of scans and tests and confirmed she had suffered cerebral haemorrhage leading to a stroke. They immediately administered clot busting medication called the tPA to try and reverse the effects of the stroke as the eligible time to do this procedure since the symptoms first showed up had not elapsed. Relevant surgeries were also conducted and in course of time, Jyotsna became conscious.

Mahesh was at her side when she was awake. Her speech was partly slurred and her left side was paralyzed. She was soon to realize her disabilities and a good deal of consoling by Mahesh and counselling by her doctors gradually retarded her delirium.

After her discharge, Jyotsna had an extensive regimen of physiotherapy which lasted for almost a year but this only had marginal relief on her well-being. It was then that Mahesh realized that her situation was something which he would have to live with probably for the rest of his life. A couple of nurses were always in attendance by her bedside to take care of all her wants and monitor her condition.

The confusing part for Mahesh was that Jyotsna could not remember what it was that had given her a traumatic experience resulting in the stroke. Also, the house helps did not find anything amiss in the room where she had the fall. They did mention to Mahesh that Jyotsna had spoken of a strange sound which she only had heard prior to her emitting a couple of loud screams. Piecing these bits of information together, Mahesh gathered that his wife definitely must have been subjected to extreme fear resulting in trauma and the consequent fall.

Once again, the service of a *pandit* was requisitioned and a very elaborate *puja* was conducted to keep all evil at bay. Mahesh also positioned two female security guards in the room where Jyotsna lay all day long for a twenty-four hour watch on her security.

Another year went by and yet there was no visible improvement in Jyotsna's condition. Then one day while the nurses were preparing to serve her lunch, Jyotsna was lying wide-eye and looking at the fan. Suddenly she shrieked and even with her slurred speech she managed to convey that there was some fearsome form on the fan which she felt had come to kill her. The nurses and the security guard came by her side and tried to calm her down but she was beside herself with fear. Her face contorted and she let out one scream after another and then unable to ward off the sinister spectacle, she closed her eyes and gradually entered a phase of deep slumber.

Mahesh was apprised of the developments and now he was certain that their house was jinxed. With a great deal of thought and advice from close relatives, he decided to shift to a smaller apartment in another building that he had built.

All was well for some time till one afternoon when Jyotsna's lunch was being laid out, the nurse in attendance was jolted by an apparent superhuman force when her hand was twisted causing the tray of food to fly off and scatter its contents on the floor. She screamed hysterically which caused the female security guard to come running to her aid but she couldn't utter a word. That was it. She packed her bag in a jiffy and took off even before Jyotsna was made aware of what had happened. The other nurse did not dare attempt to serve Jyotsna her lunch lest she have the same fate as her colleague. She watched nervously while the security guard called up Mahesh who was there in no time.

Mahesh pleaded with the second nurse not to go and leave her wife in the lurch till he made alternative arrangements. The nurse reluctantly acquiesced. Three things were now clear to Mahesh - there was no effect of the *puja* done by the *pandit*, the 'force' was stalking them irrespective of where they stayed, and thirdly, it was now attacking even those who tried to serve or help Jyotsna. He was in a quandary.

He retired to his room and sat down deep in thought. Suddenly he had a brainwave. Why not book a room permanently in a reputed hospital and admit Jyotsna so that she would always be in the care of the nurses and doctors? This would obviate the necessity of having nurses and security guards in the house, besides probably warding off the effects of the 'force' in a crowded place like a hospital. He called up his trusted friend, Sanjay, who had some clout amongst the top brass of a reputed chain of hospitals. Sanjay heard Mahesh attentively and then asked for a day's time to organize the arrangement.

True to his word, Sanjay called up Mahesh the next day and said the latter could get his wife admitted forthwith. He was even able to negotiate a very good rate for the room. Mahesh thanked him profusely.

Jyotsna was wheeled into a spacious suite with a nurse in attendance round the clock. Her condition was also being monitored periodically by the doctor on duty. It was a fair arrangement with no foreseeable hiccups as to her safety and security.

Five months passed without any incident. Mahesh was happy he had taken the right decision to admit her in the hospital. He used to visit her every day at least once and take stock of her condition.

Just when he thought everything was over as regards the mysterious force, he was summoned one night at around 2.00 a.m. by the hospital. The message was crisp – Jyotsna had suffered a cardiac arrest and was battling for her life in the ICU.

Mahesh reached the hospital in no time and was apprised by the nurse on duty on the developments. She told him Jyotsna had been sleeping peacefully when all of a sudden she started screaming and yelling, "Save me, he's sitting on my chest." She was by Jyotsna's side in a jiffy and noticed she was trying to fight off some invisible force with her right hand. She asked Jyotsna what the matter was when the latter repeated hysterically, "Can't you see him? He's trying to throttle me."

The nurse was perplexed but nevertheless joined Jyotsna in her nocturnal pursuit. She waved her hands over Jyotsna's chest but did not encounter even the semblance of any obstacle. After a couple of minutes of what seemed to be an intense struggle, Jyotsna collapsed. The nurse summoned the doctor immediately and the rest was what Mahesh had come to know from the doctor after his arrival.

Mahesh maintained vigil throughout the night but Jyotsna's case was a hopeless one. In spite of the best efforts of a team of cardiac surgeons, she passed away at 5.15 a.m. Mahesh was devastated. He wanted to cry aloud but his mouth was dry and no tears welled in his eyes. His friend, Sanjay, was there to offer him support to bear the irreparable loss and Mahesh laid his head loose on the former's shoulder. Gradually, he summoned courage and took charge of the situation.

After the funeral rites were over, Mahesh began contemplating on what his next step should be. He was convinced that no amount of security cover could fend off the effects of the 'force' if it ever chose to strike in future. However, he felt that now it was necessary for him not to stay alone but always be in the company of relatives, friends or known acquaintances. With this view in mind, he agreed to move in with his brother, Ganesh's family.

For some time there was peace in Mahesh's life. Another year passed by without any untoward occurrence. The initial fears that Ganesh and his wife, Sushila, had over the possibility of experiencing some unearthly incident on account of the presence of Mahesh in their midst were gradually put to rest and life seemed to once again move on placidly.

Sushila used to be alone till around 6.00 p.m. when Mahesh and Ganesh would be away for work. She was a strong woman, spiritually inclined and had nerves of steel. She was never one to believe in stories of paranormal occurrences which she would hear once in a while whenever she went for a vacation to her native place in Rajasthan. However, Mahesh's story seemed different, coming as it were from a near relative and the tragedies that befell the family earlier somehow gave credence to his story. Still her rational mind did not allow her to indulge in such 'trivial' distractions from prudent behaviour.

It was nearing 6.00 p.m. on a Friday evening. Sushila was folding dry clothes she had retrieved from the clothes line when she heard some muffled sounds emanating from Mahesh's room. She tiptoed to the closed door and then with a quick jerk of her hand threw it open. All of a sudden, the sound subsided. There was total silence in the room as she stepped in to see if anything was amiss.

What she beheld was enough to give the creeps to even an avowed rationalist. Mahesh's bed which had been made by the house help, after he had left for work, was turned upside down and the photographs of him and his family which had been kept atop the dressing table were torn into shreds and strewn on the floor. Besides, the impression of the right palm of an adult presumably smeared in blood was left on the mirror.

All the fortitude and courage that Sushila had garnered over the years and held close to her heart came crumbling down. With an instinctive scream that would have sent a chill down anybody's spine, she bolted from the room closing and locking the door behind her. She ran to the phone and in between hysterical gasps conveyed what she had seen to her husband, Ganesh. The latter informed her that he was on the way and would reach home soon.

Sure enough, Ganesh arrived and Sushila took him straight to Mahesh's room. It was exactly as she had stated – the bed was all topsy-turvy and the imprint of a blood-stained palm was still on the mirror just as the torn pieces of photographs lay scattered on the floor. Ganesh surveyed the scene and his face became pale. How was he going to resolve this new affront to their otherwise peaceful existence? The thought was uppermost on his mind as he followed his wife out of the room.

Mahesh came home soon after and then a frank discussion of the unholy incident and its fall out on the lives of Ganesh and Sushila took place and, at the end of which, Mahesh decided that he would revert to his two-bedroom apartment. He did not wish to put the lives of his brother and sister-in-law in jeopardy.

So, the following day, Mahesh returned to his home and decided to stay put and cross the bridges as they came. His apartment was on the topmost floor of a twenty-five storied building and had a small terrace area abutting the master bedroom.

That night, Mahesh did not sleep expecting something to happen. But the night passed off peacefully and also several nights thereafter, causing Mahesh to believe that he had finally got rid of the menace, whatever it was.

Some months elapsed and then late one night he felt uneasy in the belly and woke up to drink some water. Almost instinctively, he felt the presence of some being around him. He switched on the light but there was no one, nothing at all. As he hit the sack again, he heard a thumping sound in the terraced area outside as if someone was walking with heavy steps. Jumping up in a trice, he went out and looked around. It was a full moon night and the terrace was bathed in the beauty of the celestial light. As his eyes roamed the full length of the terrace he noticed a figure, rather an apparition, at the far end leaning against the edge, much the same way he had seen a silhouette a couple of years back in his penthouse. He felt a chill go down his spine but mustering some courage he took slow steps towards the strange phenomenon.

As he came closer, he could see that it was the apparition of a man probably in his thirties. He had bloodshot eyes, was clothed in a white shirt and *dhoti* and seemed to exude the fury of an aggrieved person.

Before Mahesh could speak, the apparition began, "*So we finally meet, isn't it? You do not know who I am, but I know you, you miserable wretch! You have yet not paid for the cruelty of all your actions but you will do so tonight. People like you who live in opulence at the expense of the sweat and toil of poor and unfortunate lesser beings without even caring for their well-being are blood suckers and do not deserve to exist in society. That is why you had to lose your son and wife in traumatic circumstances. Every day that you breathe, a poor family somewhere, whose lot it is for you to support, is left homeless or without nourishment. What can a poor labourer who works for you do but look up to you for succour? And when that is spurned by you, the retribution that would be forthcoming would be beyond your scope of endurance. This is what you have invited for yourself and you will have no chance to prevent the consequences of your actions."*

Mahesh was tongue-tied and could only cower in fear. Something told him that his nemesis was at hand and he would be fighting a losing battle trying to confront and thwart it. So he thought of taking the alternative course, that of running for his life. He had turned to do just that when he felt a great force pulling him by the collar of the shirt and then finally lifting him. In a moment he was on the edge of the terrace wall shaking with extreme fear and unable to even let out a yell as he saw very minute automobiles pass by on the thoroughfare over 250 feet below.

As the apparition tipped him over, he thought of his family for a moment before his body landed on the car park of the building in a bundled maze of flesh and bones covered in a pool of blood.

The spirit of Birju had taken vengeance and its mission fulfilled, his soul could now rest in peace.

THE END

7

The Amulet

The amulet dazzled from inside Kanta's jewellery box. Her four-year-old daughter, Parul, climbed onto the bed nearby, wide-eyed and excited at the brilliance that the jewellery radiated. Even for her little brain, the display of so much yellow metal coupled with her mother's delicate handling of the various pieces, conveyed the message that something really valuable was being examined. So, obedient that she was, she perched herself on a pillow at a fair distance of five feet away from the scene of brilliance and from thereon, surveyed the jewellery in wonderment.

Kanta was busy picking up each item of jewellery and then after donning it appropriately on her being, stood in front of the full-length mirror to view the effect. One by one, the pieces adorned her body and each time it seemed that she made a mental calculation as to which pieces would complement each other when worn in tandem. During one such embellishment, Kanta spied the wondrous gaze of an innocent Parul eyeing her every movement.

"Do you like mama's jewellery, my doll?" she asked affectionately.

"Hmm," pouted Parul, her amazement getting the better of her vocal abilities.

Kanta picked up a small bangle that she had bought for Parul and went over to where her daughter sat on the corner of the bed.

"Try this on, Chippy," she said. Chippy was Parul's nickname given by Kanta.

Parul extended her hand as Kanta slipped the bangle effortlessly past the chubby palm and onto the tiny wrist.

"There. Doesn't that look nice on you?"

Parul looked up with glee and made an ecstatic sound in agreement with her mother's contention.

"Is this for me, mamma?"

"Of course it is, my dear."

"When I grow big, this bangle will not fit me. What then?"

Kanata was nonplussed by this sudden observation from her daughter. She gave her a sidelong glance in amazement. "I will buy a bigger bangle then for you," she said affectionately, giving Parul's chubby cheeks a harmless pinch.

"Like that, isn't it?" said Parul, pointing to the solid gold amulet, shaped in the form of a thick arm band resting in a corner of the rectangular jewellery box.

"Ha, ha, ha, that's an amulet my dear, to be worn on the arm of a big person, an adult, like your daddy or me. A bangle is always smaller because it is worn on the forearm," she said, touching the precise area on Parul's arm where it would be worn.

"Oh, I see," remarked Parul, with a reflection of the situation as if coming forth from a matured person.

"This is how it has to be worn," said Kanta, as she proceeded to demonstrate how the amulet was to be worn on an adult's upper arm. Parul watched in awe as the thick amulet shone on her mother's arm. "This is a piece of jewellery that has been inherited by your daddy from his daddy, who, incidentally, received it from his mother. So, it is a family treasure, understand?"

"Oh," exclaimed Parul, with a gleam in her eye which suggested that she had appreciated everything that her mother had said.

"The amulet is expected to bring in good luck to our family, so it has been for generations," said Kanta. Parul gave a smile and nod of her tiny head as an indication of understanding what 'good luck' was.

Kanta finished her examination of the jewellery and then re-arranged all the pieces once again in her jewellery box. Parul clambered down from the bed and she and her mother made their way to the drawing room where Kanta's husband, Parmesh, was reading one of the three newspapers that were dropped every morning on their front porch. Parul ran to her dad and curled up on the sofa beside him. Parmesh gave her a warm hug and continued reading the paper. Parul picked up the plastic building blocks that were lying on the floor and once again sat beside her father to assemble them as she thought fit.

"I've been trying out all my jewellery and I feel I won't need to augment my stock for some time to come. I have already decided on the pieces I'll wear for Kiran's wedding coming up in November," said Kanta with a sigh of contentment as Parmesh looked from above the newspaper at her.

"That's very reassuring. It relieves me of the boredom of having to cart along with you in your forays at various jewellery showrooms," said Parmesh, with a smile that spoke volumes of having been divested of the onerous responsibility. "But, of course, I'll still have to be bothered about the occasion when you would be going to select your saris, etc., I guess."

"Oh, come now, don't look upon my shopping sprees as being a source of drudgery for you," replied Kanta, as she picked up a building block lying under a sofa and gave it to Parul.

"So, what are we having for dinner?" asked Parmesh. "I'm hungry and want to sleep early too. I have a tough day ahead tomorrow. Two meetings with principals, a tender to finalize and a wedding of an office colleague to attend later in the evening, is quite a handful for anyone."

"I've made *parathas* and vegetable curry with wafers and sweet pickle on the side," replied Kanta.

"Sounds yummy to me, let's eat."

Parul kept her creation on the sofa and followed her parents to the dining room. Parmesh sat down at the top of the eight-seater dining table, with his daughter and wife seated on either side of him. He was the chief operating officer of an FMCG firm and had a job which involved a lot of travel around the globe. Even while in India, his days would be stretched to the limit before he would have to perforce close shop to be with his family. It was a delicate balance that he had struck over the years, between office and home, which had now become a part of his daily regimen.

Parmesh had come up from humble beginnings. A brilliant student who had studied over candlelight in a tiny village in Rajasthan, he struggled to overcome all odds before being absorbed in mainstream white collar employment as a management trainee in his present firm. Over the years, he had progressed in the organization by sheer dint of hard work and, of course, being noticed by the right people at the right time, to reach the higher echelons of management and finally as the number two in the company. People commended him on his abilities but as his parents were wont to say that besides his effort, there was the hidden hand of luck extending from the amulet which was tucked away in the inmost recesses of a large steel cupboard in his bedroom.

Kanta, too, had reportedly benefited from the effects of the amulet being in the possession of the family. From a sickly creature suffering from leukemia to becoming a perfectly healthy woman, her cure was dubbed by many in the medical fraternity as a miracle which had no precedent in living memory. But people in the family and her relatives in the know of things accepted that her transformation had everything to do with the enormous powers of the amulet, which had come to be known as the well of good fortune.

Even for Parul, it was diagnosed at the time of her birth that she had a heart valve problem which would have required surgery at a later stage. But, over the years, this condition got corrected by itself in literally inexplicable circumstances.

The story went that Parmesh's grandmother's husband was an erudite lawyer who had an extensive and lucrative practice at the Supreme Court. In one of the cases which were referred to him, a wandering medical man was accused of having administered some herbal drugs to a woman to cure her illness, on account of which it was alleged by the prosecution that her condition deteriorated, finally resulting in her death. Parmesh's grandfather defended the accused and, after a protracted legal battle which had caught the nation's attention, he finally obtained the acquittal of the medical man. Later, a review petition in the same court was quashed for want of any legal basis.

It was a new lease of life for the medical man. He thanked Parmesh's grandfather profusely who, unfortunately, was a victim of a road accident soon after. Nevertheless, to register his gratitude for the deceased lawyer, he handed over a solid gold amulet to Parmesh's grandmother which, according to him, had unbridled powers to bring luck and well-being to the possessor of the same and all ensuing blood relations and individuals by marriage. But, he claimed, that should it fall into wrong hands either by way of theft or loss, it would bring enormous harm to such illicit holder of the same. Parmesh's grandmother was a trifle reticent to accept the strange gift from the medical man but, on the insistence of her son, that is Parmesh's father, she condescended to retain it in her small bundle of personal belongings. And so the amulet came to be recognized as an important and inseparable source of luck and success, besides being the purported panacea for illnesses and other ailments.

So the amulet was indeed a storehouse of luck and fortune for the entire family that extended from the blood relations of Parmesh's grandmother and father to individuals who were entwined in their fortunes by marriage. It was, therefore, not without reason that Parmesh had insured the solid gold heirloom from all possible causes of damage and loss, albeit at a hefty annual premium.

A week into the month and Parmesh was all set to travel to the United Kingdom to meet some vendors of food ingredients. During his absence from the house for five days, Kanta decided to bundle Parul and leave for her parents' home about twenty km away. The mother and daughter had a change of scene which was refreshing and Parul, especially, revelled in the company of her grandparents, who showered her with love and affection. But little did Kanta realize what was in store for her on her return, for fate had cast a shadow over her household.

For on entering her house a day prior to the arrival of Parmesh from abroad, Kanta was shocked to realize that the house had been burgled and besides cash and other documents, her jewellery box, and with it the amulet, had been stolen from the massive steel cupboard where it had been held secure over the years. Kanta sat down in despair with Parul beside her as the saliva in her mouth dried up making it difficult for her to even utter a cry of help. She informed her parents who came immediately and they jointly went to the local police station to register a complaint of theft and loss of valuables. The police came immediately and conducted their preliminary investigation after which the insurance company was also informed.

Parmesh arrived the following day and was dismayed to learn about the turn of events. However, as advised by the police, he decided to bide his time and wait for some promising news in the progress of the investigation.

Weeks and months passed and then a whole year went by and yet the police had not been able to crack the case. The investigation changed hands a couple of times and the new investigators again raised their volley of questions to Parmesh and Kanta. It was becoming a headache to answer queries again and again, without a solution appearing in sight, but the couple maintained their composure in the hope that, one day, the case would be solved. But, it was their wishful thinking after all for much as they prayed and hoped for a closure of the case, the police were unable to gain fresh ground and then, with the passage of time, both Parmesh and Kanta decided to move on with their lives and soon forgot the travails that had come their way with the loss of their valuables, especially the amulet.

Meanwhile, the miscreant who had burgled Parmesh's house was in dire straits. Within a month of the burglary, he lost his parents in a train accident and later in the year, his ancestral home in a small village was burnt down in a forest fire. His son died of an electric shock and later his leg had to be amputated on account of gangrene. The sudden rush of misfortunes in quick succession made him consult an astrologer who, after doing his preliminary studies, concluded that the burglar was in the possession of an item which he had obtained lately, which was the purported cause of all his troubles. After a careful analysis, the astrologer concluded that it was the amulet and advised the burglar to dispose it off as soon as possible to prevent any further damage. The burglar did as advised and sold the item at a ridiculously low price to a renowned jewellery showroom.

True to its properties, the amulet wreaked havoc in the business of the jewellery showroom. The sole proprietor died soon after, leaving a void at the helm of affairs. His family was clueless about the business model and soon their next of kin took over the management leading to suspicion and doubts in the conduct of the business which easily gave way to friction, acrimony and finally ruination of the entire clan. The business died a natural death and was bought over by another jeweller who, after a careful analysis of the sequence of events leading to the downfall of the family of the earlier owner, concluded that it was the amulet that was at the centre of all the calamities. He promptly sold the amulet to an auction house at a fair price and his action bore fruit, for the newly-acquired jewellery business rose from its ashes like a sphinx.

Very soon, the amulet went under the hammer in a foreign land and was bought after robust bidding by a wealthy individual who preferred to remain anonymous.

Meanwhile, Parmesh, on the retirement of the chief executive officer of his company, took over his mantle after the board had elected him unanimously to the post. His responsibilities increased manifold as did the expectations that the employees had of him.

One day, he received a letter from one of his close friends who was residing in France. It was a very sentimental letter, one that would have touched the heart of anyone reading its contents. For, in it, Parmesh's friend, Suryakant, had stated that his health was gradually deteriorating and his family too, was not looking very good. He stated that ever since he had left Belgium after ending his business there and decided to settle down in France, he had encountered failing health and even doctors were at a loss to diagnose the exact nature of his ailment. In the circumstances, therefore, he requested Parmesh to meet him at least once before it would probably be too late to do so.

Parmesh was overwhelmed with emotion after reading the letter and, after informing Kanta about it, made preparations to immediately fly to France and meet his friend. Within a week, therefore, he had arrived in France and then he was at the bedside of the frail-looking Suryakant. The latter clasped Parmesh's palm with deep affection as tears welled up in his eyes. For a moment, neither spoke before Parmesh reassured his friend that everything would be okay in God's good time. Suryakant's pent-up emotions gave way to a wail as Parmesh consoled him with ceaseless reassurances. Meanwhile, Suryakant's wife and two children arrived on the scene and it was evident that they were also not in the pink of health.

Suryakant's brother was also residing in France and it was on his insistence that he had decided to close shop in Belgium and move to France. Now, it was his brother and his family who were taking care of him. After sharing some pleasant moments based on past memories, the family and Parmesh sat down for dinner after which they turned in for the night.

The next day, Parmesh was taken on a tour of the spacious bungalow and the precincts thereof. After seeing the whole estate, Parmesh's eyes rested on a golden object kept inside a thick glass case on a mantelpiece in a corner, at the top of the stairs within the bungalow. The object was glowing on account of a bright light focused on it and looked quite majestic, even in the relatively insignificant area where it was placed. He went over to it and examined it closely. To say that his eyes popped out of their sockets in amazement would in itself be an understatement; for, ensconced within the glass case was the long lost amulet which was once his possession. He turned towards Suryakant, wide-eyed in disbelief. Seeing his astonishment, the latter gave him the semblance of a smile and was about to explain the circumstances by which he came in possession of the object.

But before he could begin, Parmesh blurted out, "How did you get possession of this?" he asked, pointing at the amulet.

"Just before I left Belgium, I had attended an auction and this amulet was up for bidding. I instantly took a liking for the item and mentally decided that I would bid successfully for the same, whatever be the damages. So, notwithstanding the stiff bids that were emanating from various quarters, I stayed the course and finally succeeded in making the highest bid after which the auction for the item ended. I was handed over the amulet and I came home victorious like a general in battle in ancient times who would have garnered the spoils of war. Soon, thereafter, my family and I moved to France and I had since encased the amulet as you see it now," said Suryakant, with a gleam in his eyes.

"No, no, you mustn't keep it any longer. Every moment that this amulet continues to remain in your possession, you and your family will experience destruction and doom in your fortunes and well-being," exclaimed Parmesh to a bewildered Suryakant. He then set about to explain the entire history of the amulet to his friend, at the end of which he had to help a gaping Suryakant to a chair positioned nearby. The latter did not speak for a while, so struck was he in wonderment.

"You mean to say that this amulet could be the cause of all my troubles?" queried Suryakant, amazed to the core.

"Yes, precisely, since it has the powers to bring widespread misfortune to anyone in its possession other than its original owner, which is me," replied Parmesh, emphatically. "I suggest you hand over this amulet immediately to me so that your family and you will no longer be susceptible to its ill effects; but, of course, I shall compensate you with the exact amount that you had paid for the item in the auction at Belgium. Please do not misunderstand me. I am doing this for your good."

Suryakant had no doubts on Parmesh's integrity. Strange and mysterious though Parmesh's story of the amulet may have seemed, he knew that there was not a shred of untruth in it. He had known Parmesh too well since their childhood days to have even a shadow of doubt on his friend's narrative. While he stood there and insisted that Parmesh take the amulet with him without any compensation, the latter would hear none of it.

"I don't want you to suffer a loss. It has to be a win-win situation. You get back the money you paid for it and also a complete relief from all its retrogressive effects and I and my family once again become the recipient of its bountiful effects as it was originally meant to be."

Without further ado, Suryakant applied the key to the lock of the glass case and requested Parmesh to take out the amulet with his own hands. Parmesh did likewise and signed a cheque for the amount paid for it in the auction and handed over the same to Suryakant. The deal was over and the amulet was restored to its rightful owner. Almost instantaneously, Suryakant felt a tremor within his being and a sudden burst of energy. His fatigue seemed to be getting transformed to exuberance and he felt the blood surging in his veins. All of a sudden, he began to feel that he now had a reason to live. His wife and children had also experienced a turn for the better and came to Suryakant to break the news. Suryakant was now convinced beyond any doubt and he thanked Parmesh profusely for his help. The latter acknowledged with humility the praises showered on him and said the whole episode was engineered by the hand of Fate and he was only an instrument in the whole process.

The following day, he bid goodbye to Suryakant and his family but not before receiving a commitment from him to pay a return visit in the immediate future. Suryakant was only glad to agree.

Parmesh returned to India and on reaching home, he announced to Kanta, "I've brought you a wonderful gift, something you can never imagine."

"What on earth could that be?" she asked.

"You just bear with me a few seconds," said a beaming Parmesh, as he unzipped his suitcase and delved his hand into a corner. In a jiffy, he was holding the amulet before her eyes.

A shocked Kanta was unable to take in this sudden development. She slumped into a sofa and glared at her husband in astonishment. Then her questions came in a flurry. "Is it our lost amulet? Is it the same? Where did you get it from? Did the police retrieve it from the burglar or did someone hand it over to you, or did you find it somewhere by chance?"

"Hold on," said a smiling Parmesh. "This is indeed the same amulet, our amulet." He then narrated what Suryakant had told him as Kanta heard him in utter amazement.

"What a turn of events," she said. "Indeed, fate can cook up strange recipes for all to savour in wonderment."

Parmesh and Kanta lost no time in telling Parul and all the members of their extended families the good news and then there was a grand celebration to commemorate the occasion.

The amulet was kept in a thick-walled state-of-the-art safe, specially requisitioned for the purpose, and once again insured from all damages and loss.

As for Parmesh, Kanta, Parul and all other family members, it was the beginning of a new era. There was an optimism to live life once again to the fullest and a confidence to face it with fortitude with the guaranteed protection from the mysterious amulet, a bulwark never failing.

THE END

8

The Prophecies

Sam Richardson rose from his sofa and went up a spiral staircase to the attic where a number of items which were not in use were stored. These included pieces of furniture, furnishings and artefacts, but Sam was suddenly interested in a particular item which he had hidden from the world.

It was a planchette – a simple apparatus used to communicate with spirits. It comprised a relatively thin heart-shaped wooden piece which was mounted on two wheels with the third support being provided by a pencil with its point facing downwards. At the time of obtaining this sinister piece of equipment from an auction, a demonstration of its powers was shown to Sam, wherein a person's two fingers were placed on the wood and the pencil moved automatically and registered some message on the paper held beneath. It was also presumed that the spirit controlled the psychic form of the medium.

What is it that had driven Sam to go in search of the occult piece of equipment was not clear, but there was an eagerness in his gaze as he climbed past the first and the second floors and reached the confines of the attic. He did not meander and inspect items as he passed by, but went straight to the corner where he had tucked away the planchette from prying eyes of visitors to his home. He bent down and parted the elaborate cloth covering to reveal the item. With a quick movement of his hand, he picked it up and retraced his steps. At the hallway on the ground floor, he laid it on a large piece of blank paper and looked at it intently. It looked very quaint even in the bright rays of the afternoon sun that pierced through the large windows.

Sam knelt down to engage the planchette in his intended foray into the unknown. He placed the forefinger and middle finger of his right hand lightly on the wooden surface of the instrument and closed his eyes to invoke the spirits from his ancestry. Almost immediately, the planchette began to move and the pencil in the front began writing a message on the paper below. Sam went into a trance as the equipment wrote vigorously on the paper in what seemed to be an elaborate communication of what was in store. After a while, it stopped moving and Sam, whose two fingers were all along on the item, now opened his eyes and looked at the message that had been compiled in a neat handwriting. He moved his fingers away from the planchette and set about to read what had been written; and this is what it revealed.

Before the completion of this year, you will face a tragedy in the family. One of your close relatives shall die suddenly and you will not be able to attend the funeral. Besides, sixty-six months from now, you will be struck with a debilitating illness from which you will not recover. But there is a silver lining in the cloud – in a cave, hitherto unexplored in Mt. Kapuluchi, at about a height of 2000 ft. facing the west, there lies a bottle containing an elixir, which will be a cure for your ailment. However, it is not easy to find this bottle and you would need to use all your tenacity to trace it within the cave. Even if you are successful in retrieving the bottle, you must not open the same or consume its contents till the onset of your illness. But once you have decided to drink the elixir, you must not leave the bottle unattended, even for a second. Should this happen for some unforeseen reason, the elixir would be destroyed forever and the advancement of your illness and your death would then be imminent.

Sam studied the message closely and then folding the paper neatly, kept it in the drawer of his cupboard. He was a widower, his wife and two children having died several years ago in a tragic accident in a mountain range in Kenya. Since that time, he had been staying alone in his opulent house with a team of house helps at his beck and call. He was a businessman involved in the leather trade, an occupation which took him to several places around the globe. In fact, it was his business which kept him going and prevented any sort of surrender to bouts of depression.

Sam reflected on what the spirits had said in the message about a tragic death taking place before the passing of the year. He had a younger sister, uncles and his brother-in-law and all their families. None of them were old enough to die of age-related symptoms, so it was indeed going to be a tragedy in the family with a sudden death causing a pall of gloom.

Six months later, Sam had to travel on business to Africa and just two days into his itinerary, he received a call from his brother-in-law who informed that Sam's sister had passed away after a massive heart attack. It was a great shock for Sam who used to dote upon his younger sibling. But he was far away from home and his entire trip, which included several client meetings, had been carefully planned to the last detail. To wind up and return would have been catastrophic for him as many issues would remain unresolved and hence he chose to grieve in silence and sent word that he would not be able to make it for the funeral. The first prophecy of the spirits had come true.

After he returned from his overseas trip, Sam was seized of the second prophecy which had been made out in the message and he sat down to reflect upon it. He had heard of Mt. Kapuluchi but did not know its precise location. Besides, he had never done mountaineering or trekking before and this, therefore, was an area where he needed assistance. He hired an accomplished mountaineer and together they set out in search of the mysterious elixir.

Sam and Philip, the mountaineer, reached Mt. Kapuluchi, which was about 400 Km away from home. It stood amongst a scattering of other mountain peaks and was quite imposing to the casual onlooker. They began their climb in good time and covered about 1500 ft on the first day. They found a clearing off a beaten path and decided to pitch camp. The following day, they resumed the climb and located the cave on the west side of the mountain. It was a great feeling of reassurance for Sam as the prophetic enunciations were true, at least thus far. The two men clambered up to the cave and stood outside for some time.

Philip had brought a large ball of wool, one end of which he now tied to a piece of rock at the entrance of the cave. Holding the ball of wool, he entered the dark and eerie cave followed by Sam. Both men had brought torches and lanterns which they now put to good use. The cave was quite large at the entrance but as the two men forayed inside it, they realized that it had several narrow caves within, all facing different directions which gave the impression of a maze. They went through eleven such caves without any result. Each time, the ball of wool helped them to retrace their steps and come back to where they had started.

There were still three more small caves to be explored and the men decided to complete the task forthwith. Going through the first one, Sam inspected every nook and corner but there was nothing at all. The second cave was long and meandering and the men had to go in single file. Not seeing anything even after a while, Sam was about to turn around when his eyes picked up an object which was lying in a crevice near the roof of the cave. Sam grinned as he stretched his hand to retrieve the object covered securely in a dirty cloth which he removed carefully, revealing a bottle with a colourless liquid entrapped inside.

Sam let out a cry of delight. "The elixir, the elixir, I've found the elixir," he exclaimed. Philip gave him a grin in acknowledgement.

"Yeah, finally our exploit has been productive," he remarked. The men retraced their steps with Sam holding the bottle tightly in his palm. It was past noon when they began their descent and reached the foot of the mountain before dusk.

Sam reached home around midnight. On the way, he bade goodbye to Philip and thanked him for his assistance. Sam placed the bottle in a corner of a steel cupboard, where he normally kept all his valuables.

Days passed and soon years went by. Sam had marked out the month which had been alluded to by the prophetic message, when he would be stricken by a debilitating ailment and knew the time was fast approaching. He visited all his close relatives, lest he be denied a chance later on.

When eventually the fateful month arrived, Sam was in jitters. He tried to deflect his mind from the impending ailment, since he was still not sure of the efficacy of the elixir, by involving himself in various pastimes besides his regular work; but when the sickness finally struck, he was suddenly rendered vastly decimated in his various faculties. Even so, he stumbled to his cupboard and, after retrieving the bottle from within, went to the dining area where he placed it on the table. He looked at the bottle closely. There were no markings, nothing at all, just a clear colourless liquid, filling about three-fourths of the bottle. The message by the planchette had mentioned that the elixir should not be left unattended once he had decided to consume it. Sam gave the bottle one long, hard look before he reached forth and opened the cap. Inside, the liquid gave out a musty smell. It would be a nightmarish experience to consume the liquid, he thought, but he had no option. So, holding his nose with the forefinger and thumb of his left hand, he raised the bottle to his mouth to drink the elixir in one go, when, all of a sudden, his landline began ringing. In that suspenseful moment, the sound was very sinister. As if by default, Sam placed the open bottle on the table and went to attend the phone in an adjoining room. It was an overseas call from one of his key customers. He sat down on the chair next to the phone and resigned to hear what the caller had to say.

Meanwhile, through an open doorway, a black cat entered his home and after scampering here and there, reached his dining table upon which the open bottle containing the elixir was standing. It jumped on to the table and, in a bid to explore the contents of the bottle, toppled it with a small thud. The elixir flowed out and spilled on the floor. The cat smelt it then withdrew and made a dash for the door but not before Sam saw the feline creature dart across the floor, its distinct glassy eyes looking ominous in the reflection of the light. He returned to the dining room only to be flabbergasted at the spectacle before him. The elixir lay splattered on the floor.

Seven days later, a senior house help informed one of Sam's uncles that he had passed away in his sleep.

When the house was put up for sale, all the prospective buyers were put off on seeing a black cat perched on the compound wall with its sinister eyes penetrating their very being.

As for the planchette, it was discarded in a garbage dump from where it was picked up by a rag-picker and then, of course, the story of another prophecy was ready to unfold itself.

THE END

www.ingramcontent.com/pod-product-compliance
Lightning Source LLC
Chambersburg PA
CBHW020326180726
47991CB00019B/866